A CHANCE ON CHRISTMAS

KIRAHVI BELLO

OTHER TITLES BY KIRAHVI BELLO

The Book at the Bar Series

The Book at the Bar

Hooked on You

Standalone

A Chance on Christmas

BEFORE YOU READ!

This book contains themes of Instalove, age gap and explicit sexual scenes. The story follows a widower finding love with mention of topics such as spousal death in the past (not on page).

Please take care of yourself while reading.

A NOTE FROM KIRAHVI

Hey there! I'm so excited for you to read my Christmas novella. I hope this book brings you hope, comfort and excitement. Christmas is my favorite time of year and I'm glad to share this book with you.

I ask that as you read, keep your mind and heart open. What may seem unrealistic to some, may very well be someone else's life.

May you enjoy your holiday season to the fullest. I can't wait for you to read Vernon and Tishelle's story. I hope their love impacts you the same way it did me.

This is a work of fiction and should be enjoyed as such.

Thank you Reader!

Kirahvi Bello

A CHANCE ON CHRISTMAS PLAYLIST SOUNDTRACK

For a great listening experience, please click the best link to access the playlist on Apple Music or Spotify or scan the most appropriate QR code.

Apple Music Playlist

❄

Spotify Playlist

Winter Wonderland by Warren Wolf
Sleigh Ride by Johnny Mathis
Warm in December by Samara Joy
The Happiest Christmas Tree by Nat "King" Cole
Happy Holidays to You by The Whispers
Share My World by Mary J. Blige
Slow Down by Mary J. Blige
Uhh Ahh by Boyz II Men
First Time by UNV
The Closer I Get To You with Donny Hathaway by Roberta Flack
Share Love by Boyz II Men
It's Beginning to Look A Lot Like Christmas by Leslie Odom Jr
My Gift to You by Alexander O'Neal
A Colorful Dream by David Bendeth
This Time of the Year by The Whispers
Christmas Blues by Eric Reed
Snowflakes of Love by Toni Braxton
Be Mine for Christmas Ft. Ledisi by Kem
Silver Bells by Coco Jones
Our First Christmas by Alexander O'Neal
I'll Be Home for Christmas by Al Green

This Christmas by Stephanie Mills
Baby It's Cold Outside ft Louis Jordan & His Tympany Five by Ella
Fitzgerald
What Christmas Means to Me by Al Green
Black Christmas by The Emotions
A Marshmallow World by Darlene Love
Lovin' You by The O'Jays

1

TISHELLE

"If one more man asks me to pay for another date, I swear I'll just pay for my food and leave." I told my best friend, Lashai, on the phone. "I'm tired of men wanting to be treated like princesses. He expected me to pay for *both* of us. His profile said he was a contractor and when I asked him about his latest project he said he hasn't worked in six months because he's turning down gigs."

"Wait, he said *out loud* that he's purposely turning down contracts? Is he hurt or something?"

"No! If he were sick or just got out of surgery, that would make sense. He's just ignoring all of his contracts because he says he hasn't felt like working and didn't have a back-up plan. His parents offered to pay for his rent, instead of him earning his own money. I should've run then, but the food had just come out and I was stuck. Then for the rest of the date he said he's looking for someone he can be 'equally be yoked' with. Like... zero plus zero is still zero, dude. I'm deleting my dating apps. I'm so tired of wasting my time dating. I wish I could get reimbursed. Why did a piece of food fly out of his mouth mid sentence?"

"Ew that's your pet peeve."

"Exactly! I didn't even want to eat anymore."

"I hear you, sis. Are you still going to that business meet and greet at the coffee shop close to you? It looks like it could be fun."

I buttoned my navy blue blazer; business was slow during the holiday season but rent still needed to get paid. The New Year brings fresh ideas and I want to be the first thing on the clients mind. I need to be engaging, convincing but not pushy-*such a delicate balance for a black woman*. "Yeah. I'm getting dressed. I have to get clients somehow. Business has been slow but I'm good to take care of myself for now."

"We get it, Ms. Independent. I can't make this one, but I'll be at the next. I need to get this house together for dinner on Sunday."

"Ooo, let me come through and get a plate tomorrow."

"Fine by me, less sitting in my fridge to go bad. You know I don't eat leftovers."

I rolled my eyes. In all my years of knowing Lashai, it had been me getting thick from clearing out her fridge. I've never had a meal that I didn't love from my best friend. I might get her another cookbook for her birthday, though she could probably write her own.

"Shai, when are you going to write that cookbook? You experiment in the kitchen anyway. Just write down what you do, take some pictures, and be done."

Lashai sighed, "Okay Ms. Agent, I'm not one of your clients. I don't feel like doing a damn cookbook. I have enough on my plate as is. I don't even have a restaurant, why would anyone want to buy a book from me?"

I began filling my Coach purse with my phone and wallet. "It ain't nothing to create an audience. I had an author as a client a few months ago and helped her market her next book. I can connect you with a ghostwriter."

"I love you, but I'm not applying for Sweet Honey's Marketing Agency just yet. Mmkay?"

I blew air from my nose. "Yes ma'am, just trying to help my best friend be even more awesome than she already is." I jingled my keys, put on my shoes and was about to walk out of the door. When I touched the front doorknob, it jiggled because a screw was loose. Was it safe? No. Have I put in tickets and told the leasing office about it? At least 5 times in the past two months.

"I'm so tired of this damn place. I'm gonna have to show my ass the leasing office if they don't fix the stuff in here."

"Girl, why can't you just fix it yourself?"

I slammed my front door and locked it. "Because the last time I tried to fix my tub, I made things worse. The hole is getting bigger and I'm scared of mold. That's why I don't want to own a home yet. Too many DIYs."

"Well if you let *real* men come by, instead of the YNs, a grown man might fix it for you so you don't have to wait."

I sighed louder as I got in my car. "So you're saying I need to stop dating younger guys?"

"YES!"

I sucked my teeth. "I'm sorry that when I get horny I want to get put through the headboard. Somebody's grandad can't do that."

Shai laughed. "Tuh I bet he can after he that takes that Viagra, I bet he'll lock you in. Remember silver fox? I still call him every now and then."

I connected my phone to my car's Bluetooth as she continued. "He was on some other shit the last time he came through. I'm still stretching. The trick is, making sure he's working out and taking his vitamins. You know how essential vitamins are after 30."

"Girl... I love you but I can't stand you. I don't want to take care of an old man that looks like a raisin." Lashai would never give additional information about 'Silver Fox'. I was starting to believe he was a myth. I don't want wrinkles, I want to see abs and get picked up. Granddaddy can't move that good.

"Hey, while you try to get me to write this cookbook, I'll try to get you to get with a man that will treat you right. You're thirty-two now babe. You hit your Jesus year this year and I want you to be happy. Maybe talking to a different crowd is what you need. Not all men are perfect, but I think you can find the one."

"Jesus year? 33? You have been hanging around older men too

much." I put the coffee shop into my map. "I don't actually feel like being social. Maybe I could just go to the park or something."

"First off, at least I'm getting some so don't try to come for me and my jokes." She chuckled. "Are you not wearing the suit you *just* bought? It's got good luck on it, and it makes your ass look great. I'm sure people will be throwing their business cards at you like ones in *Blue Flame* if Atlanta won a Championship."

I laughed so hard. This suit did make me look good, that's why I hoped my credit card would take the charge, surprisingly it did.

"Just go for an hour, collect some cards then go about your night. You might walk out with a client."

I twisted my lips, trying to find the business agent inside of me. "Right! I've already got pamphlets and packs of thank you candy on me too."

"So you're ready! Call me after if you need it okay? I'm still expecting you for Sunday dinner tomorrow so I'll cook a little extra."

My mouth watered thinking about Shai's Sweet Potato pie.

"Is it okay if I ask you some questions about your business? If you haven't already, we can create a marketing plan leading to your launch. I have a free template that I can send with customizable options so every post can be tailored to your target audience and gain you followers," I said with a playful shrug. "Love it or hate it, still free."

She gasped, "Wait, really, girl? I am clueless with this stuff.

"One of my most successful clients was able to triple her sales and book out her schedule for the next eighteen months. Great marketing, pushes you into the right hands," I added extending by business card.

"I thought people didn't like business cards? I thought QR codes were the thing."

I agreed. "They are! But people still like to have something to hold, so having your information as a take away is helpful." I flipped the card other show the QR code on the back.

She studied me with interest and extended her hand, "Lemme see your card. I'll need to catch up with you. I'm trying to hit *that* next level."

I handed her the card a bag of mints, tea, and other assorted candy I had prepped with additional information.

"A little Christmas pack, too? Alright now, I see you."

I made my way around the room; some people were in a better mood to talk than others. I didn't mind. I can make peace with knowing I tried my best and put my best foot forward. You can't undo a first impression.

I sat at the counter with another hot chocolate in my hand and it was just warm enough to make me feel cozy, but not sleepy. *Time for me to head out and get back in my pajamas.* My hope of Christmas dick has been depleted.

"Excuse me, is someone sitting in this seat?"

I turned around to be greeted by a young man with a large smile, "No, it's free actually."

"Great!" The man beamed. "Sit here, baby." Then, a woman with a sleeping baby in her arm sat down next to me as the man helped her.

"Thank you!"

I nodded standing up. *Yea it's time for me to go.*

As I was walking out of the door, I felt a small tap on my arm. "Hey, I'm here for the networking event, but I'm confused about who's participating and who's not. Are you here for it?"

I'm wearing a suit, who else would wear a real suit on a Friday night in a coffee shop? "I am. Or at least I was."

He looked sad for a hint. "I'm sorry, I don't mean to hold you. Have a good night, ma'am."

I gave a small smile. He had a salt and pepper beard with warm, deep brown eyes. He was slim but not quite skinny. He smelled good, almost close to cinnamon. His bone structure was nice with cut cheek bones. He looked cute, but definitely older. I wonder what brought him here. I looked down at his clothes and saw he had on a tie with... reindeer? It was dark green and they looked like they were flying. Where do you even buy a tie like that? A Christmas market? I thought about turning away but I changed my mind. I need to know about this tie. Christmas is an eh holiday for me right now. I can't afford real gifts, so there goes my holiday spirit. But his man proudly approached me. "Are those reindeer on your tie?"

"Yes, they are! I have the whole group, Dasher, Dancer, Prancer... Sorry, Christmas is my favorite holiday so I can go on about this tie. I'm Vernon."

He extended his hand and I shook it firmly. "I'm Tishelle. Christmas is okay but I don't do extra. I might have one sweater, maybe, that I wear every other year for work but I haven't seen it in awhile."

He shrugged, "I've embraced it more since my daughter moved out. That's why it's been more affordable." He chuckled to himself, "Tell me about yourself. I'd love to hear about your business."

I put on my million dollar sales smile. "I'm in marketing, specifically a product specialist. I work with entrepreneurs and small business owners to take their product to the next level. What do you do?"

"Oh," he looked around like he was trying to find an answer. "I work for the city in water management."

I raised my eyebrows and narrowed my eyes. "So you were there when the fiasco of no water downtown happened. People were hot about the Meg concert being delayed."

He sighed loudly and held his head. "I was there on the front lines, helping put down new pipes. Anything to help get everyone back on track. The Mayor had to come out and everything. Do you want to sit down and talk more? Are you finished with your drink?"

I shook my cup, it was empty. "I can go for another hot chocolate with oat milk."

He smiled so big that it made me smile wider. As he went to get our drinks, I claimed an empty table for us in the corner. He came back.

"So, Ms. Tishelle, are you from Atlanta?"

I nodded, "I am, actually. Born and raised here, even though it's rare since so many people move here. My mom used to live off of Ralph Abernathy."

"Wow! I'm from here, too! It does seem rare nowadays. It's crazy to see how much it's changed throughout the years."

"I feel the same. I hate the gentrification, I'm tired of seeing townhomes around every corner. I remember when there used to be trees. Now, if a corporation sees an empty lot, townhome, townhome, houses cramped next to each other." I rolled my eyes.

"Me too, as good as this growth is in some ways. Not the best building choices have been made. It hasn't made my job easier either."

I glanced at his tie again- it really had reindeer on it. I would never wear something so cheesy, even if it is Christmas. On him, it's actually cute. "I'm sorry if I'm staring but I still can't get over your tie."

He pulled it out, "Yea my daughter and I would wear different sets on Christmas day to be fun. She thought matching was 'too much' as she got older, but I held onto it."

"I am in the "too much" crowd," I chuckled. "I don't have one decoration up."

He did a fake gasp that made me laugh. "Not everyone keeps a Christmas tree in their home and work office."

I raised my eyebrows, "Wow, really? Like a real tree?" I think I ran into a real Christmas fan.

He laughed quietly to himself, "Yes, that is something, I have to admit. I'm hybrid, so I don't do much in my work office. I do have a little tree in the corner at home that I decorate throughout the year."

Aww, throughout the year. "That's cute! My tree isn't even up in my apartment."

His eyes widened. "But Christmas is around the corner? It's December, Tishelle. Where will Santa leave your gifts?"

I shrugged, "I haven't even thought that far in the future." I need clients so that I can have a comfortable future, not living on Lashai's couch.

I'm surprised I didn't glance at my phone, or daydream out of the window. Talking to Vernon was engaging and never ending. Before we knew it, a random bell rang, "Well folks! We have hit the end of our event. And it looks like someone is under the hidden mistletoe."

The room turned and shifted their gaze to Vernon and I. We looked up and saw a plant with a small red ribbon tied, hanging in the air above us. *How did I miss that?*

"We don't have to do anything," Vernon said in a hurry. "I've talked your ear off already."

I blew out air. "This is probably the closest I'm getting to a Christmas kiss." I shrugged leaning in towards him for a kiss. Vernon chuckled and did the same. I was going to turn so he kissed my cheek, but I want to see what our kiss would be like. Our lips meeting in a light and quick peck, along with the growing excitement in my belly. His breath tasted like coffee and mint, his lips were soft and hesitant as his mustache brushed my nose.

I pulled back with a smile, "Not bad, Mr. Vernon."

He admired me, "Glad you chose to kiss me." The room applauded as we awkwardly got out of our seats. "May I walk you to your car?"

I was taken aback. I didn't know guys did that anymore. "Sure."

We walked through the parking lot to my car. It wasn't a far walk, but it was dark outside, so I'm glad he offered. I unlocked my car and he opened the door. "May I give you my card? It has my office and cell number. We can see each other again to talk socially or professionally. It's been nice speaking with you tonight."

I took it and handed him my card with the pack of candy. I read his full name and put the card away. "Mine just has my office number, but it forwards to my cell. I'd love to connect again."

A friendliness shined in his eyes. "Me too. Drive safe, Ms. Tishelle Walker."

"You too, Mr. Vernon Carpenter."

At home, I sat on my couch, looking between the empty corner where my tree usually goes and Vernon's business card between my fingers.

"Hmm, I would be open to something more social." I said to myself.

We kissed, and I wanted to *keep* going, not in front of everyone. but it woke me up. I was so horny that I was humming for any type of action. He was cute, and he looked at little older, but not like a grandad. Just some cute salt and pepper in his beard.

I called his cell and he answered on the 3rd ring. "Hey, Ms. Tishelle."

Umm, how can I say this without sounding thirsty?

"Hey, I was just calling to get on your schedule for a, um... meeting. I had a great time meeting you tonight."

"Would it be professional... or social? Just so I can know how to dress and where we should meet."

I chuckled, "Would you mind if it was social?"

He hummed. "Of course I wouldn't. How about we meet tomorrow at 7? I'll text you the address. Does that work?"

Oh, he just took the reins with planning. I could get used to this.

"Yes, it does. I'm looking forward to it."

"Me too, Ms. Tishelle," his warm voice purred on the line before hanging up. After making sure the line was dead I exhaled.

See, that wasn't so hard? It's just a social date close to Christmas, nothing crazy. *But the big question is what am I going to wear.* I quickly stood up from the couch and dug into my bedroom closet. I needed a dress to show my figure, but not all my cleavage.

2

VERNON

She said yes.

I have been blessed with the opportunity to take Tishelle on a date. I'm glad my reindeer tie caught her attention. I chuckled to myself as I drove home.

I thought I would come off unprofessional asking her out at a networking event, but she actually agreed. *I need to make this really special.* I've been on dates since Beatrice died, of course, even sexual ones. It just didn't feel the same. I'm not looking for a woman like Bea, there is no one else like her. I just hate online dating; seeing someone eye to eye is important. I thought dating nowadays wasn't for me and I was okay with that. Until I saw Tishelle, beautiful, determined, focused, prepared. I'm looking for a woman that can hold her own so that I can support her and her dreams. Tishelle seems like she could be that woman.

I don't think she understood how she looked floating around that room with her infectious smile. The holiday's used to feel sore with memories, but my daughter, Genesis, would always uplift my spirits. I never realized how lonely I was until she moved out for college. She's not far, only a couple of hours away, but still. My home is becoming a museum of memories. Beatrice made me promise to not stay in the house if I didn't want to. My bedroom, Beatrice and I'd old bedroom, has been packed for years since I moved downstairs.

I just need a push. One final push to call my realtor. Genesis would hate me, but I'll tell her about it after Christmas to not distract her before finals. Our house is the only one she's known her whole life. We bought it when Bea was four months pregnant. We barely had time to move in all of our few belongings, but we were happy.

I got home and looked at the rooms upstairs, filled with packed boxes. Most of it can be donated, I don't need to keep holding onto everything, just the parts that bring the best memories. I just haven't had time to go through everything again. I want to live somewhere smaller, so I don't need to keep holding onto everything, just the things that hold the best memories. I want to cherish each day I have like Beatrice wanted me to. Now, to make sure my suit was clean for a great second impression for Tishelle.

The next morning, I sent Tishelle the information for the restaurant and where to park. I was so nervous, I dyed my beard back to black and gave myself a fresh line up. *I know she's younger than me, but, Lord, if it's in your will, please allow this to go well.*

I sat in the parking lot 30 minutes early, so I knew I wouldn't be late. I said another silent prayer, gently grabbed the bouquet of flowers I hoped she would like, and began to head inside.

I have to take this chance.

I have to take this chance.

3

TISHELLE

Vernon @6:55pm: Here in lobby

I EXHALED AND GOT OUT OF MY CAR. MAYBE I SHOULDN'T HAVE WORN this dress. It was black, silky, and had an open-back. I have a few rolls, but I'm a human that likes to eat. If he finds me unattractive, I'll immediately turn around and leave. I'm keeping my eyes open for red flags. You can see a man's true interest in his eyes.

I walked into the lobby to see him in a slick black suit, holding a bouquet of bright red roses with a green ribbon tied around the floral wrap. He had a wide smile on his face

"Good evening Ms. Tishelle, these are for you."

I accepted them and held them in the crook of my arm. I haven't received flowers in so long. This is a social date, but maybe it can turn romantic.

"Thank you so much, Mr. Vernon."

The server escorted us to a table near the window. When he pulled out my chair, an approving moan escaped his lips. *He must have seen the back.*

"Your dress is beautiful and you look radiant."

I'm glad I went with the open back black dress. The roses complemented the color so well and we were matching. Like a real couple. He gave me a look in my eyes as he sat down.

"These flowers truly are beautiful. I can't remember the last time I got flowers that I didn't buy myself."

"You're welcome. I wanted to make a good impression for our *social* date."

I blushed. It was working on me.

"I appreciate the thought. Do you buy flowers often?"

"For my daughter, Genesis, yes. She's away at school, but I still send them to her dorm every now and then so she knows her old man is thinking of her. I used to keep fresh flowers in the house when my wife was alive."

My eyebrows raised. It was the first time I've heard of a wife while on a date. But the 'alive' part shifted my thoughts.

"Oh, I'm sorry for your loss. How long were you married?"

"Almost 14 years. We got married in 2003 when we found out she was pregnant. We were only dating for a few months, but I felt I was ready to step up to the decision we made. We bought a house soon after and tried our best to join our new lives together. I was 25, and I knew that I wanted to be the dad I never had. Truthfully, I wasn't the best man when we first got together. I still had some growing up to do, I can acknowledge that now. She passed from cancer 8 years ago, Genesis was 14 when she passed so she remembers a certain ideal of her mother."

I swirled around the wine in my glass listening. He's an open book.

"Does Genesis know that you're dating? Is this your first... date?" I can tell already he spoils his little girl. If she's not braced for him at least looking for a relationship, no matter how old she is it would be a shock. I never want to make him choose me over her. But I need to be important too.

"I dated again after she graduated high school," Vernon explained. "Some were serious, but I wasn't ready to be married again. They never seemed like the right one. I've been on dates here and there, but none had that..." he eyed me, then met my glance. "That something special."

I welcomed the burning in his eyes. "Well I've had my fair share of sorry dates without that 'something special'. I can't seem to meet the right one either."

He lifted his glass to me, "To new beginnings."

I raised mine as well. "To new beginnings."

We sipped and made approving faces of the champagne. The conversations in the restaurant were low and the lights were dim, but I still took a look around. Everyone was dressed in formal attire like us, and there was a bar on the other side of the room.

He spoke again, "How old are you, If you don't mind me asking? I know you are younger than me."

I studied him. "I just turned 32 last month, on November 21. You?"

He chuckled. "47."

I tried to hide the shock on my face. I knew that he was older than me from the sprinkles of grey in his beard, but not that much older. Black really doesn't crack. 20 years ago I was 12 years old and he was 27. Not a questionable gap cause I'm grown, but, *hmm*.

"Does me being almost 50 scare you, Ms. Tishelle, sweetheart?"

I giggled looking away. "No, of course not. Age doesn't always mean maturity. I still agreed to go out on this date. I peeped your grey, even though you dyed it away. You don't have it hide it from me. I still agreed to go out on this date. You don't look your age at all." I bashfully smiled at him. "I've been single for a while, so I'm open to broadening the dating years. We've been having fun so far right?"

"I definitely have. I get to gaze at your beauty. Was it a New Year's resolution? Broadening your dating years, I mean."

I shook my head. "No it just happened that way. I find you... attractive."

He made a charming face, "Attractive? I like the sound of that."

I rolled my eyes. "See, now I want to stop puffing your head up with compliments."

He brought his hand to the table, motioning towards mine. "May I?" he asked. I nodded, and he took my hand.

There was a still moment where he just looked into my eyes and I looked into his, reading his soul, trying to solve his mind like a Rubik's Cube as his thumb brushed against my palm. I could feel his eyes on me as I watched him play with my hand. The way he traced the lines made goosebumps rise on my back.

Let's see how the night goes.

"What would be your dream Christmas gift?" he asked before taking another sip of wine.

I moved my lips. *Should I give the real answer or say something basic?*

"Do you want the real answer or a typical answer?"

"Real. I always want you to be real with me. I hope to gain your trust so you never have to hold back." He met my eyes like he was reading my soul, waiting and listening like I was about to say the important thing ever. I sighed and gave in.

"I've always wanted a necklace with a T. Growing up, people would call me Michelle, and I got so tired of correcting them all the time. I always wanted to wear a T, so that I could point and say 'T as in Tishelle.' I know it's stupid. I never got one, and when I got older, I didn't need it. This may be random, but I also wanted a Dooney & Bourke purse. My mom had one and it made me *so* jealous."

He nodded, listening intently. "Well, Tishelle, I'll make sure any and everyone will call you by your name. And you can never go wrong with a quality purse."

The server took our food orders, refilling some of our wine.

"What would your dream dessert be darling?"

I thought for a moment. "Okay, good question. I would want a bowl of cookies and cream ice cream with extra crushed-up Oreos, and a few whole ones to eat while I scoop. They're my favorite thing ever. If I had a bad sweet tooth craving, I'd would pour chocolate syrup on top." He laughed with me.

I hoped I didn't sound annoying, but I can go to a good place or bad place when chocolate and Oreos are involved. There are just some sweet things I should eat alone, and that is an Oreo. I'm good for opening them, licking the icing, and then eating the cookie. Mr. Vernon would probably lose his mind if he saw me licking anything. I want to see him lose his mind on top of me.

Focus.

"Have you tried the Cakesters?" he asked, sipping his wine.

"I have! I just ran out, too, and wanted some more. They're so good and soft. They're even better with a sweet white wine." I groaned louder than I probably should have just thinking about them.

"What's your favorite dessert, Vernon? Do you still have some... guilty pleasures?"

He licked his bottom lip. "I don't feel guilt for any of my pleasures. But I do enjoy something sweet every now and then." He eyed me like he wanted a taste, I gave him the same look back. "I would say a slice of pound cake fresh out of the oven with some vanilla ice cream."

"Mm, I love me some pound cake, especially with strawberries."

As we waited for our food to arrive, he told me about what Genesis was studying in school, and I spoke to him about the adventures Lashai and I had in college

"What's a fun fact about you, Vernon?"

He shrugged, "I can drive a stick shift. I used to have a real nice Cadillac. Man did I love that car."

He then shared a full smile that put his pearly white teeth on full display. How did that make him look finer?

"I bet driving in traffic with it was fun."

His lips twisted. "That's why I got rid of it. Atlanta traffic wasn't always this bad."

We laughed harder together. He turned his head to the side for a moment, revealing piercing holes on his left ear. There's a story there and I'm curious to hear it.

Our conversation was like a well-played game of tennis: he would flirt with me, and I'd send a hint back. It was sexy talking to someone that could keep up with me. Our orders came, a plate of steak, broccoli and mashed potatoes for me and a lobster risotto for Vernon. We even talked about everything, from our favorite historical landmarks in the city to Genesis' messy roommate. We were laughing so loud that some of the other patrons would look over at us. This was the best steak I had ever had. It was earthy and melted on my tongue like butter.

When I look into his eyes, I just trust him.

This is different and nice.

"I'm so full. I hope you still find my full belly pudge attractive." I scoffed, pushing my plate away.

"Sweetheart, I find your laugh, personality, and body attractive. You are gorgeous and confident. I can see it in your walk. You have a power and confidence people would envy." He reached across the table and lightly kissed my knuckle.

I giggled and looked down, not pulling my hand away.

"I saw you working the room before I got to you. Then when you finally sat down, I could tell you were thinking about something. I was just hoping to catch you before you left. I had to at least introduce myself."

I wrinkled my nose. *Oh he was scoping me out.* I'm glad I caught his eye. I lifted the bouquet he bought me and met his eyes as I smelled them, then placed them back down. His eyes danced around my face. Even though we met at a business focused event, I'm open to keeping this going.

I sighed, "Somebody else would have been scared to approach a woman like me. I was ready to leave, when that guy asked if the seat was available I took that as my notice to leave. I thought I was talked out, but I'm glad you stopped me. I'm definitely having fun with you tonight."

We chuckled. "I felt the same. When you're behind a desk a lot, it feels good to go to those events sometimes. It reminds you about what's important in businesses: the people you serve."

I nodded in agreement.

The server came with the bill and it didn't even touch my hand. He extended his hand for the check while reaching into his back pocket. He pulled out cash and gave it back to her. I reached for my wallet to give the server a tip.

"Why are you taking out your wallet?"

"To pay the tip since you paid for dinner."

He shook his head in disappointment. "Look here, baby, you don't need to take out your wallet around me. I'll take care of you." He gave me a look as I put my wallet back into my purse. I wasn't going to argue about that.

He walked me out to my car and I didn't know whether to hold his hand or lock my arm with his so I just held my purse close to me. Maybe he couldn't tell I was nervous. "I had a great night. Thank you."

He tipped his head, "You're welcome, beautiful."

As he was about to turn away, I gently touched his elbow. The contact shocked me while making my stomach roll with excitement.

"Would it be appropriate to ask for a kiss goodbye?"

He smiled and took a step closer to me. "Anything for you."

I placed my arms around his lean shoulders and leaned up to reach his lips. The kiss started as a light peck, us navigating our own anxiousness. Then, when I felt his length grow between us, something in me ignited. I opened his mouth with mine and began exploring with my tongue. I thought he would pull away, but he pulled me closer as his large hands cradled my lower back, his thumb brushing my exposed skin.

Go lower... go lower.

I continued to kissing him as I pushed my breasts into him more, pushing higher on my toes to get closer to his mouth. I could feel my thong getting more soaked as my nipples hardened. I moaned and began winding my hips onto him. I knew I shouldn't have gone on a first date while ovulating, but, damnit I want some dick. I stopped our kiss and gave him a light peck on the cheek.

"Want to go back to my place?"

He removed his hand from my back and lightly massaged my

hips, slowly bringing his hands up my sides. "You want a late night coffee, gorgeous? Something hot and burning for you."

I kissed his jaw. "More than coffee. I want the sugar with extra cream."

"Oh I got it for you baby, whatever you want."

"I want to give you everything I got," I said with a gasp. Then I kissed him again, this time deeper. I gripped the collar of his shirt for leverage and his hand slipped behind me and rested on my ass. Then he began rubbing and squeezing as his hand crept down the back of my dress. I start spreading my legs wider as his fingers work their way down, squeezing my ass on his way down to my wet lips. I shivered as he opened me more.

I'm so fucking glad this is open back.

He made his way down until he reached my pearl, going in slow achy circles, using his other fingers to open me more.

"You like that?" he whispered against me.

I could only gasp against his lips. I needed to sit in his lap before the end of the night. I dragged my hand from the front of his shirt down to buttons to his belt.

He groaned and slowly pulled his hand from my dress. He was about to brush my juice on my lips but instead he licked and sucked his finger with a louder moan.

"You said your place?

"Yea I can... I can send you the address." I could barely think straight with him still standing so close to me, smelling so good, smelling me on his lips. If I didn't pull away now I'd be bent over my backseat.

He opened my car door and I got in, connecting my phone, checking my purse and turning the car on. Already forgetting the most important thing.

"The address, baby? Unless you changed your mind I don't want to force you."

I was taken out of my trance. "I'm sorry, I zoned out for a second." I quickly took my phone out of my purse and texted him.

He smiled when he heard his phone go off. "I'll see you in a few babygirl."

"See you," I sighed.

I wonder what his face will look like when it's in between my legs, his hair peaking out as I spread wider for him.

I'm about to find out.

4

TISHELLE

I BEAT HIM TO MY PLACE AND IT FELT LIKE I WAS THE ENERGIZER BUNNY. Should I shower? Would he want to? Should I just pounce on him? What if I came on too strong? I only had 2 glasses of wine and so did he so I'm not drunk. The kitchen was clear. My room was spotless. I put on my playlist so I can tear him apart as soon as we get there. I also lit one of my favorite candles, I would vacuum but I don't want to miss the sound of his -

Knock. Knock. Knock.

I jumped and tried to hide my surprise. I was so nervous, but I needed the cob webs knocked out of me. I hope I don't break this man's back.

I walked to the door, still dressed in my dress, without my heels on. I didn't notice the true height difference between us before. I'm 5'6" and he's at least 6'3".

I gave him a sly grin. "Hey,."

"Hey, beautiful. Sorry it took me longer. I went by the store for a few things."

I noticed the white plastic bag in his hand when opened the door wider to let him in. What could he have gotten from the store? Some aspirin?

"What did you need?"

I swung my hips as I walked and tapped my nails on the dining table so he could empty it in front of me.

"At dinner you mentioned running out of your favorite snack, so I got you some more." He took out a pack of Oreo Cakesters.

I did a little shimmy as I picked it up. "Ah! I forgot I even said that. Thank you. Is that another box in there you're trying to hide?"

His eyes didn't leave mine as he placed a large black box onto the table, a box of Magnums- XL.

"Oh, damn." He wasn't shy about it at all. "So you wanted to make sure you were prepared."

"I'd rather have it and not need it, than need it and not have it."

The side of my lips lifted as I sauntered over to him before placing a light kiss on the corner of his lips. "I have some, all you had to do was ask."

He stroked his hand up and down my back. "I didn't want to assume."

I glanced at his lips and leaned up on my toes. His nails brushing my skin excited me so much. Our lips met again with more hunger I was about to push him onto the floor when he pulled back. "Can you sit on my lap facing me?"

Intriguing.

"Yea come here." I guided him to the closest chair with his back against the dining table. He moaned his approval as I hovered over his legs, careful not to put all of my weight onto him.

"You can put it all on me baby, I can handle it."

I sat on his lap and rested my arms on his shoulders.

"Good girl. Mmm, I hope you didn't mind me rubbing your back all night. It's so sexy."

He brushed his finger tips up my spine as I licked his neck. "I like to be, teased with touch. You can have your hands on me, anytime."

He kissed under my jaw. "Teased with touch. I like that."

He brought one hand to the crown of my neck and gently squeezed while the other was brushing my waist. I leaned my head back, opening my legs wider on his lap. I opened my mouth as chills spread around my body, his fingers on my scalp holding me steady. I looked back down and met his eyes. We were in a trance of passion, drunk on each other. I slowly stood up, brushing my leg and foot against him.

I grabbed his hand, leading him into my room. He seemed curious at first and then intrigued. My comforter and sheet set were peach and pale yellow with four pillows perfectly arrange on top of them. I had photos displayed in a far corner near my vanity. My peach rug covered the area around the bed. The vanilla scented candle made the room smell amazing and the music was just loud enough to set the mood even more.

"I love your room. It's almost as cute as you."

I chuckled as I closed the door behind him. "Thank you," eying him hoping my eyes gave him the invitation to come closer to me.

He obliged, and his hands found themselves caressing my sides as we began kissing again. I slowly lifted my hands to unhook my dress. When the fabric fell, brushing in between us, his eyes followed. Vernon pulled himself closer to me while grabbing a hand full of my ass, kissing around the crux of my neck.

Vernon's hands paused over mine as I started to unbutton his shirt.

"I didn't catch you off guard did I?"

"No sweetheart, it's just been a while."

"Oh." I stepped back and began to cover myself, looking for my robe. "I'm just getting naked, tearing your clothes off. I'm sorry. I didn't mean to be moving so fast…"

Right before I stepped away, his hand grabbed my naked waist, giving reassuring brushes of his thumb. "I didn't say to move, I just said that it had been a while. You're so picturesque, I lost my words. You're more than beautiful. I don't want to rush my intimate time with you. Every moment you're in front of me, I want to cherish it. I want to cherish you."

He took off the rest of his shirt and pants, wearing nothing but a black tank top and briefs. His body wasn't bad either-not too skinny, but enough to have some hidden muscle. When I brushed my hand against his stomach, I was met with abs. I looked up at him and bit my lip as he led me to the bed.

"How about I give you a massage to make up for it?"

I handed him the lotion on my nightstand. "I accept."

He got my chair in the corner and brought it close to the bed. He sat down and rubbed his thighs guiding me to sit on his lap, facing the bed.

"Do you want me to lean forward on the bed?"

"Yes baby," he lightly kissed my lower back.

I brought a pillow so I could lay my head on it while his legs were securely under me, like I was sleeping on a desk in school. But a fine ass man was about to rub me down.

"I know this position is different, but trust me."

I put my head down on the plush pillow and took a deep breath, breathing in the vanilla scent filling the room. With my back facing him, he had all access to me. I heard him pump the lotion into his hands, rub it onto his hands, then onto my back. I thought I enjoyed the here and there touches from our night tonight, but to feel him intentionally rub into my curves, rolls, and kiss up my spine? Unmatched. I wasn't scared to have my full weight on him, and began to push myself further back.

When he reached my neck, one hand gripped the back, and it made my levy break as he squeezed.

Give me more.

I brought his other hand to my breasts. He groaned as he massaged both, welcoming the guidance. I slowly rolled my ass on his growing erection. Anyone else would've just rubbed my clit twice and fucked me. Vernon makes more goosebumps rise just from how he reached and grabbed my other breast. He touched me like it was the last, like time was moving too fast and he wanted to savor every second and minute of tonight; like it was the last time. If he wants to take all night sending voltage through my body, I'll take it. The pressure on my areolas made me rise higher and higher.

I groaned louder and fell back onto him as he felt down to my stomach. His thumb brushed the bottom of my chin as he turned it to place a kiss on my shoulder. I squirmed, squeezing my thighs together trying to please the ache.

"I'm here with you baby. I'll take care of you." His hand passed my pudge, opened my lips and guided gently to my clit, drawing small circles and giving light squeezes.

A growl rose from the depths of my chest, and I spread my legs wider to give him more access. My soaked sounds filled the room as he played with me. I squeaked as Vernon slipped a finger in, feeling him spread me wider with a second finger.

"You're so tight, baby. You've been waiting a long time for me?"

"Yes. What took us so long to meet."

Vernon plunged me fast with a twist, unforgiving and intense, then slowed his pace back. With my climax still rising, he read my skin like a book as he kissed my ear sending waves throughout my body. "That's it, baby, that's my Tishelle. You look so beautiful. Give it to me, give it to me. You can trust me."

I yearned for his command and strong voice, and twitched and turned my waist on his lap until I squirted. My juices soaked his briefs and my rug. I was panting, still trying to catch my breath.

"Fuck," I said in between breaths. "That felt so good." I ran my fingers through my hair. I need to be filled more.

"I want you feeling good all night, sweetheart."

I moaned and turned around standing, and began to pull his briefs down as Boyz II Men played.

"You don't have to worry about me."

Vernon was on full display in my face. I began feeling him in my hand; he was stiff as a rock, pointing directly towards my mouth. With a slow lick, I pushed him deeper and deeper past my lips. His head fell back as I started slowly, pushing him further down the back of my throat. I looked up to see him staring me in my eyes as his jaw dropped. His hand massaged the back of my head as he tickled the back of my throat. I sucked from the bottom, pulling out his early excitement.

He jerked his dick back as he took a step away from me. "Mm, those lips, baby. You are too good. Come here."

He helped me stand up and pulled me in for a kiss, not light, but messy, licking his precum from my mouth. I slowly lifted my leg against him as he picked me up and placed me on my back on the bed. My hand grazed the back of his ear and his tongue caressed mine in return. When I felt the pillow behind my head, he bent down and licked my nipples as he made his way down to my stomach.

Vernon blew a cool air on my lips before slowly lifting my legs, holding my thighs open.

"So beautiful baby."

I couldn't take another breath as he devoured me. His tongue danced and plunged into me as I gripped his hair. He groaned like he was eating Christmas dinner.

"You taste so sweet, baby."

He lightly sucked my clit as my toes curled and cracked. Then he undid me with a trick he did with his tongue. My body filled with fireworks as I finished again on his face, my legs shaking.

"Baby baby," I groaned.

He did one final slurp with a devilish grin as he got off of the bed and went into the kitchen. I could hear him tear open the box of condoms. He came back into the room with a few packs, placing all but one on the nightstand. He then sheathed himself before getting back onto the bed.

I positioned him between my legs and looked him in his eyes as he gazed at me, his full beard still drenched and shiny. He bent down and kissed me slowly as he slid inside, inch by inch, by inch. The deeper he got the more he filled me. It was a welcome pain; it felt like he was spreading my insides and hitting my spine. He stroked me so good I could only moan and whisper his name as he smiled, kissing me each time his name left my lips. "You want it faster or harder, sweetheart?"

"Faster," I whimpered, gripping onto the bed as his speed increased, holding on for dear life. "Ju-just like this."

"Mmmhm," he rolled his hips again and dug even deeper into me as I screamed. I slowly moved my hand down his back to his ass, gripping as he continued, his sweat falling onto me. This was the kind of dick that would have me sprung, stalking him outside of his job, wearing his clothes around the house. He's fucking the shit out of me and I'm taking it all.

"Breathe. Let it go," he growled as I tightened and came again. I thought he pulled out for a break but no, he just lifted my leg and hooked it on his shoulder. *Damnit.* He moved his hips more, giving me more, fucking me more. He growled again.

"Finish for me. I know you're close."

The noise that rose from his chest to my ear made me shiver. He pulled out with a moan. "I'm not a cursing man, but, fuck. You feel amazing, Tishelle, I could be buried in you all night." He slowly stood up. "Where are your towels?"

"The hallway closet. Grab the black ones."

He disappeared and came back with the towels, placing one under me and then dropping the used condom into the trash can in the corner.

"Are you a cuddler?" I asked. Not everyone was nowadays. If he left right now ,I couldn't even be mad.

"I am. I'd love to hold you right now."

I tried to hide my smile as Vernon got under the covers with me. His fingers rubbed my thighs and back with my head on his chest. I closed my eyes as I listened to his heart beat, smelling his skin.

Please don't move.

Being skin to skin with him felt like the recharge I've waited for my whole life. No phone, no TV show in the background, just music and our breathing. After our moments of silence together, I decided to ask a question.

"How did you like everything? I didn't mean to start so fast, but you fucked me like you had something to prove."

He gave me a reassuring squeeze. "I hated to stop your head early, but I was not trying to finish too early. I do appreciate the compliment, I haven't heard that in a long time."

A long time? "So you're not being intimate with anyone else right now?"

I couldn't look him in the eye right now, but I needed to know. "No, I haven't been in a committed relationship in two years."

I hummed in agreement. "I haven't been in a real relationship in a while either... I'm glad. That means I get to have you to myself."

I looked up and saw the fire in his eyes, welcoming me. "You can have me as much as you want. As long as you know, I'll always want you too."

I brushed my hands down his chest, going past his curly body hair to his length. "Even now baby?"

He picked me up from my waist and back, laying me on top of him. "Whatever you want."

He reached for another condom on the nightstand and quickly sheathed before I lowered myself and rode him like his dick could solve all of my problems. I bounced like this was the last dick I was going to get for the rest of my life.

I need it and he won't ever forget it.

When I woke up, my thighs were tight. My bonnet sat half way off my head with a towel tucked between my legs.

Great night.

I reached to my side, expecting to feel Vernon, but was met with the feeling of my other pillow.

He must have left.

I sighed loud as I sat up in bed sore and satisfied. "Damnit, well I guess I'll never hear from him again."

As I swung my legs over the bed, a smell hit my nose. Breakfast? I slowly stepped out of my room and into the kitchen to find Vernon in nothing but briefs, mixing a bowl of grits with a smile.

"Good morning sweetheart."

I smiled and then covered my mouth as I yawned, "Good morning. I thought you left?"

He shook his head, "No, I had some groceries delivered so I could make us some breakfast. Are shrimp and grits okay with you?"

I walked around the corner and kissed his cheek. "It is. No allergies here."

He turned his head and caught my lips in slow kisses, my taste still there.

"You look just as beautiful now as you did last night and the day we met." His lips tasted like butter and seasonings as he kissed me again.

I chuckled against his lips, "You mean three days ago?"

I walked past him and made my way to my fridge for a bottle of water. When I opened the door, it was filled to the brim with food and drinks. Ground beef, chicken thighs, tomatoes, greens, strawberries, grapes, orange juice, apple juice. I haven't seen my fridge this full in... a long time. I haven't been getting many clients lately, so I've been living out of Shai's fridge and whatever I could pull together with ramen.

"When you said you had groceries delivered, you didn't say you filled my fridge to capacity."

"Didn't I tell you already that I want to take care of you? I want you fed. You don't need to worry about your fridge. Are you allergic to anything I got?"

I was dumb founded. I did not expect him to do that. I must have really bounced on that thang. "I don't have any allergies. I appreciate this a lot. Thank you, boo."

Then I glanced at the counter and saw that the flowers he got me for our first date were trimmed and placed in a vase. I looked at the flowers and back at him, and I could see him smile as he turned around.

I sat at my dining table, wavering as I slouched in the seat, "I see you're an early riser. I thought you would be more tired last night."

He chuckled. "Since you slept well, that means I did my job well."

I pressed my lips to hide my smile. He opened my oven and pulled out a fresh tray of warm croissants. Then, he dabbed a butter honey mixture on them and began fixing our plates. My stomach growled as he set the bowl in front of me. These weren't small baby shrimp, but jumbo, and seared to perfection. He even placed a small cup of sauce.

"Do you want anything to drink?" he asked.

"Yea there's some orange juice in the fridge. And could you bring me a bottle of hot sauce?"

He fixed our drinks and brought them to the table, then set down the bottle of Louisiana Hot Sauce. He placed his plate down at the seat across from me and extended his hands. I took them, with no question.

"You mind if I say grace?"

Oh? A praying man? "No, of course not."

We bowed our heads.

"Lord, thank you for this meal. I pray it provides us with proper nourishment, in Jesus' name, amen."

"Amen," I agreed. I tried to hide the confusion on my face. He really is a different breed.

When I took a bite I groaned, reveling in the buttery, savory grits and shrimp. How long was I sleep, because it's only 9 in the morning? I dipped the shrimp in the butter sauce and moaned again, pouring it over the grits. I didn't even realize my eyes were closed until I opened them to get another bite. I looked up at Vernon and he had a full, cheesy smile.

"I really like this butter sauce. I'm also super happy that these grits are savory."

"I don't like sweet grits. I wasn't raised on em."

"Me neither." We continued eating in silence between the enjoyable bites. "What are you getting into today?" I asked.

"Well, first I'm getting my toolbox from my truck to fix your front doorknob, the grout in your shower, and the shower head. They both seem really lose. I can come back to fix that light, or whatever else I find in here that needs to be worked on."

My jaw dropped. "You'll fix it today?"

"Of course. Soon as I finish eating. It's not safe for the doorknob to do that, and I know your showers haven't been comfortable."

Tuh. We'll see about that.

"Okay I'm cool with that. I've put in ticket after ticket online and nobody has even come over to fix it. It's been so annoying. I hate this complex."

He stood up from the table wiping his lips. "I'll be right back." He went into the room for a moment, then exited, dressed and went out to his truck.

Did I watch him from the window? Maybe. I thought he would've laid on the couch and cuddled a little bit before getting started.

He came back with a different shirt in one hand and a toolbox in the other.

"Need any help?"

He eyed me up and down with a smirk. "How about you fix two glasses of water and leave one for me? Drinking you up is enough for now."

I laughed. "You got it."

Seeing him go into the bathroom with a tool box and his glasses on made him look so cute. I tried to leave him alone, but I couldn't help but to peek into the bathroom and watch him work. I felt like I could watch the muscles flexing on his back for hours as he was inspecting the tub and the tile. When I came in again, the shower head was off soaking in a container.

"Hey, whatcha doing now?"

He wrapped tape around the pipe, "I'm just reinstalling your shower head. They didn't even put plumbers tape on here, that could mess up your pipes more. But I took care of that. Your shower head needed a good clean too that's why I have it soaking. I'm not putting it back on though, I'm headed to the store to buy you another one with a filter. My daughter liked it, so I got it for the house. She used it in a hotel or something. Anyway, I'm getting you a good one, not the cheap stuff they have in here. You can leave the old shower head for when you move out."

"First breakfast, now new shower heads? How did I get so lucky?"

He chuckled. "I told you I cared about you last night. I want to show you that I *can* take care of you. You deserve it. I've been enjoying my time with you."

I bit my lip. I'd call this love, but it's way too soon. I'm falling so hard right now.

"It was, I really enjoyed myself. I hope you did too. You got me so full I'm ready to go back to sleep."

"Lay down, baby, I got this. Before I give you something to make you lay down. You can relax when your man is around."

I chuckled and walked back down the hallway, laying in bed. He started playing music and I nodded along reading a comic. After a few minutes I decided to sit in the living room and watch what I could.

After an hour passed, we rode to the store together for more supplies. I almost forgot the rush of being in public and holding someone's hand. I even learned a few things as he showed me the different door knob options. The new shower head was already was making my life easier. The water pressure was stronger, and it felt amazing on my skin.

5

VERNON

Waking up today made me miss Tishelle ever more. Her laugh, her smile, her hair. When I saw how empty her fridge was, I had to take care of it. She doesn't know it, but she already has my heart. I want to see her again, but don't want to smother her. I would invite her here, but I would have to explain too much. Like why my bedroom has been packed for months and I've been sleeping in my office.

I want to start over again. Tishelle reignited this feeling in me. I started house browsing months ago, but I haven't put in any offers. I've maintained my water heater and faucets, and everything is brand new. I even updated the downstairs bathroom a few years ago, so there's extra value there.

But I need to downsize. I'm tired of cutting all this grass. I've been alone for so long I've gotten used to it. I want to be in a new clear headspace for my new future. For Tishelle.

I kept scrolling, the next house is my next new chance.

6

TISHELLE

I RUBBED MY FINGERS THROUGH MY OLD-ASS SILK PRESS. IT WAS sweated out past the point of return. After Vernon came and fixed almost everything in my apartment, I thought he was going to visit the leasing office to rip them a new one. I just finished washing my hair; the new shower-head did make a difference. I never even thought about getting a new one.

Once I started to twist my hair, I decided to give Vernon a call.

"Hey, sweetheart," he answered cooly. "How are you?"

"I'm okay... just working on my hair trying to prep my arms." I sighed loudly, my voice trailing off. I put him on speaker while continuing to work on my hair. "There is something else on my mind. It's nothing, it might be too much."

"What's wrong?" Hearing the concern in his voice made my heart swell. "Why do you sound like that? Anything I can do?"

I might as well say it and sound completely dick crazy.

"I'm just missing you and it's only been a day." We sent good morning texts, but I still wanted him next to me, kissing me. I am sprung. I hope I don't come off thirsty. If he gave a bullshit response, then I'd know the kind of man he was.

"I miss you too sweetheart, I was scared to admit it, but I was looking for you this morning. Let's go on another date, when are you free?"

I looked in the mirror, gauging the progress of my twists. *Eh I'm halfway.*

"I can be ready by 6pm. I'm working on my hair."

"Perfect, we can go to this Christmas Market in Buckhead. They have a huge tree, different stores and shops with great food. Have you ever been?"

I pulled up the event on social media. It looked fun and packed. "I think I've heard of this, but I've never ben. Let's go!" Of course my 'Christmas tie cutie' finds the cute things around town.

"Dress warm. It's outside and I don't want you freezing." Another date planned and in the book, and now I have to think about another outfit.

By the time our phone call ended, I was finished with my hair. He had to hang up to mow his lawn, and all I could think about was how much I wanted to watch him ride a lawn mower wearing nothing but a straw hat, shades, and shorts. I would sit on that porch in winter, summer, spring, and fall, just watching a black man sweat over his own land. I would answer the phone like, 'Girl, Vernon's about to cut the grass, imma call you back.' It makes no sense for him to be in this much shape. I stretched my twist past my shoulders, admiring the mirror. Vernon had no problem scheduling dates and making what he wants clear. It seems like he wants me for me, not just the ass I threw at him like a hot and ready pizza on a Friday night.

HIS TRUCK WAS AT MY COMPLEX AT 5:55PM AND TEXTED. WHEN HE SAW me exit my apartment, he got out and opened the door for me. When we arrived at our destination, he held my hand, helping me out of the truck.

"I can pay for parking," I said optimistically. "I have a good $20 in my account". I want to contribute at least something.

Vernon gave me a confused face. "I already told you to put your wallet away. I don't even want to see it unless someone asks for your drivers license. You are being funny." He did something on his phone, and my phone's notification noise dinged.

"You sent me $200 for whatever I want?"

"Yea or for later because I'm still treating you while we're here."

I smiled, entwining my fingers with his. I didn't realize how much I was missing out on not constantly touching someone, squeezing someone as we walked down the street.

"I want to say thank you again for fixing the stuff at my place. That lightbulb had been flickering for a while, but they never came to fix it." I haven't had many men in my apartment, but Vernon saw problems and fixed them immediately. He didn't even place another work order, he just got his tool bag and got to work.

He squeezed my hand. "You're welcome. I know it hasn't been long, but I care about you and want to keep showing it. No matter how many dates we get together. I want to show you off as my lady, because in my mind you are already."

I beamed, squeezing his hand. "Well, you're doing all the right things. You've been on my mind too and I was excited to see you again."

Public display of affection, check.

We walked down the street and saw a tarp. "Why is this up?"

When we turned the corner it was so crowded. It was like a flood of people were dropped off all at once. While we were pushing past the crowd, I held onto his hand behind him. When a break in the crowd came, he moved me in front of him. I looked at him, confused.

"I can't protect what I can't see. I need you in front of me, sweetheart." Butterflies rose in my stomach as he held my hand tighter.

Once I was inside, the holiday music was on full blast, the smell of candy and popcorn mixed with turkey legs filled the area. I wanted to browse before buying anything. Then, I saw the largest Christmas tree I'd ever seen in person. It looked like it was over 50 feet. Vernon found us an empty bench right under the tree and we sat down.

"May we take a picture?" I asked shyly, holding my phone. This needed to be documented.

"Come here."

Vernon kissed my cheek as I took a selfie. We did another one of us kissing, and then one more of us just smiling in the camera. We looked good together, his tan coat and sweater next to my black jacket. I wanted to stick my tongue down his throat, and I didn't care who watched.

"I'm going to get us some Apple Cider to warm us up, try to hold my spot."

"Who else would I want next to me than my man?"

He smiled so hard his teeth were showing as shock filled my face. *Fuck, did I say that out loud?*

When he came back 15 minutes later with the mugs, I tried to back track. "Did I say my man earlier? I meant, uhh something else."

He tapped my chin with his finger, then my nose, "Don't take it back baby. I'm your man."

Was it his touch or the cold, icy air blowing on my face that gave me goosebumps? I laid my head on his shoulder. There might be true love this Christmas, or a horrific holiday love bomb. I hope he keeps this up until the new year.

"Do you know if any of these shops give out holiday hugs? Because I could definitely use one from you."

Vernon chuckled, wrapping me in the deepest hug with a squeeze. "That was a good joke. Did you practice it?"

"I did. I thought you would appreciate it."

We heard his phone ring in his pocket. He held it up and answered, "Genesis." He switched over to speakerphone; the people had cleared around us so we could actually hear.

"Dad! How are you?"

He chuckled and looked at me like he knew what she was about to say. "Fine, and you?"

"Oh, well since you asked I'm not good because I need $50."

He started typing on his phone. "You need $50, I need some, too. Do you have money to slide back to me?" He dramatically presses buttons as Genesis pauses on the phone.

She says in a deadpan voice, "Thank you for the $100. You're the funniest."

"I love you, too. Have fun," he laughed as the call ended. "She didn't even say 'I love you back'. She's the funny one." We chuckled together. It was nice to see a man spoil his daughter. It shows how close they really are. We stood up and walked in a few circles. When we found ourselves in a hidden corner, he slowly hugged me, squeezing my ass, causing me to moan in his ear.

"This is a really cute date idea, Vernon. I've never been here before."

"We can come here as many times as you like while it's here."

"You make me cum? You always do, baby. Oh? Did you not say that?"

Now he was the one blushing. "I love making love to you, too. I want you more than satisfied every time. This will be here for I think two more weeks so we can come back again."

I bit my lip and pulled him closer, "Yea I need some more of that... loving tonight." He gave me the smoldering look in his eyes again.

"Making you smile is exactly what I want for Christmas this year, no matter how that smile comes." He lifted my chin and lightly kissed me.

WHEN WE ARRIVED BACK AT MY PLACE, I DRAGGED VERNON TO MY room, gripping him by his collar then pulling him into me. He's had me so turned on just walking around, holding my hand, the occasional kisses. I thought it would feel weird but it didn't. It felt cozy. Like we were two puzzle pieces that had been looking for each other.

I threw off my top as he quickly threw his shirt over his head and we dove into the sheets. His fingers ran through my twists and started kissing me down my face and jaw, holding me still as I tried to wrap my leg around him. From the length that met my thigh and the puddle that was sitting between my thighs, we were both ready.

Moving quicker than I thought, I got on top and slipped it in a second thought as we groaned.

Mmm shit.

His hands squeezing my waist, guiding himself deeper.

I winded my hips. "I'm sorry, I couldn't wait for a condom. I'm a bad girl. Do I get coal in my stocking?"

He met my eyes with a smile. "Oh I'm putting something in there." A grin that meant nothing but trouble grew on his face. He started pounding from under me, and I let my head lean back as he went deeper and deeper into me. I felt like he was stroking my rib cage from how deep he was. I started clenching around him. I groaned as my thighs shook. I let out a final scream as my hands dug into his chest. I ran my hand down as he quickly lifted me up, moving his hips from under me, turning to the side with a grunt.

"I'm sorry," I started. "I know we've been using condoms, and I was moving too fast."

He rolled back over, breathing heavy as he kissed my cheek. "You don't have to apologize. I had time to do it if I wanted to. Once I was in, I was lost inside of you."

He got up and went into the hall closet then went into the bathroom, bringing back a warm wet towel. "I'm grabbing a water, do you want one, too?"

"No, I'm okay, thanks." He came back into bed and held me, the only noise being the heat running and our breathing. I couldn't tell if we were both thinking about going raw from now on or what.

"What are you doing for Christmas next week?" Vernon asked me.

I shrugged. "I'm going to Shai's for her Christmas Eve dinner party. Christmas day, probably a movie marathon and video chatting my mom. She's been living in Brazil since she retired, so I don't see her in person much."

"Wow, Brazil? Why there?"

"She's always wanted to travel. She started in Germany and is working her way around the world. She's been abroad since she retired a few years ago. She sends me proof of life through pictures and postcards when she can actually mail them off. I've never known a woman over sixty to still go clubbing but that's her."

He laughed even harder, "I hope to meet her one day. She must be a fantastic woman to raise someone like you."

I scoffed. "That's one way to put it."

"Well, if you're free on the eve of Christmas Eve, I would like for you to be my date to Mayor Andre's Christmas Gala."

"Be your date? You don't think people would... talk about us?"

He leaned down and kissed my forehead, "Baby, you're thirty-two, not twenty-two. It's not that bad, and I bet we wouldn't get that many questions. Did you see people looking at us tonight?"

I gave him a look. "Technically, no. But there is literally fifteen years between us. You were born in the seventies."

He laughed so hard it shook the bed and made me start to giggle.

"Now you've got me laughing!"

He slowed laughing and wiped his eyes. "Oh, I thought you liked my expertise that has come with my age. Like when I did that trick with my tongue."

I looked up like I was thinking. "A trick with your tongue? Hm, I don't seem to remember that." Of course I remember that fucking tongue twirling my clit like a ribbon.

He bit his lip as he started to go under the covers. "I'll remind you."

He bent down back under the comforter and reminded me until my breath gave out with my hand in his hair.

Interconnected with no barriers.

7

———

VERNON

We laid together holding hands. I haven't done this in years. My previous relationship was more transactional: we texted twice a week, had sex once a week, and that was it. I didn't hold her, nor did she want to be held. But Tishelle, I'm crazy about her. Her hair, her smile, her style. The suit she was wearing was professional, but you can only hide a body like that for so long. I feel blessed to see her natural body. She looked up and noticed me already looking at her.

"From the neck down, what is your favorite thing about me?" she asked reading my face.

I thought about it. "Everything about you is my favorite thing. But if I was forced to pick, I would first say your thighs, because they are so thick and delicious."

She giggled and rolled her eyes.

"I would also say your back."

"My back? Are you serious?"

I nodded. "You have a beautiful body, and your back really accentuates it. The night of our first date, I didn't see that it was backless until I pulled out your chair. And, whew, baby, I couldn't help the noise I made."

Now she was all out laughing. "Can I be honest? I didn't know if you would like it. So when I heard you grunt I was like, 'Ooo he does like it.'"

Now I was chuckling, and I held her tighter. Of course we were both nervous back then. Was it only a few weeks ago? Yes, but I'm serious about her, and this will last past the holidays.

8

TISHELLE

Christmas was 12 days away and I needed to catch Lashai up on everything that's happened with Vernon last weekend. I can't believe I've been so obsessed with a man I've known for a week. We've been texting all day everyday, I'm even listening to more Christmas music from the songs he sent me. I know it's crazy to like him this much after knowing him for 8 days, but I still need another opinion to make sure everything that was happening was real.

Lashai hugged me as she stood up from the bench closest to the door. Her honey blonde cornrows still flawless with a long sleeve jumpsuit. We rocked a little, of course, then the server grabbed the menus and led us down the stairs. I always loved the décor here. It had hints of pink, with the moody table lighting with splashes of blue and explosive art.

I love this city.

You can get great drinks, better food, and spill any and all tea.

Once we sat down, I barely glanced at the menu before Shai grabbed my bicep.

"Okay, so, bitch, spill it. You've been smiling like a scammer, your phone hasn't left your hand even after our hug. What the hell has happened since the last time we spoke?"

I raised my eyebrows hiding a laugh. "You don't want to wait until the food comes? Or our drinks?"

She dramatically leaned closer with a confused face. "Does it look like I want to wait? Only thing I have to go off of was the post on your story wearing your little sexy outfit, like I don't know that's your *freakem* dress. Who is the man and what happened?!"

I looked around and leaned forward. "Let's just say he got... acquainted with every fucking inch of my skin. He rubbed me down so good and gentle, but fucked my shit up." Just thinking about his hands up my back, his lips on my ear, his tongue circling my -.

"Oh, so backs were broken. Did he stay the night though?"

I nodded, licking my lips. "I woke up to shrimp and grits with croissants fresh out the oven."

Lashai pursed her lips, "That's not toast and little ole jelly."

I slammed my hand on the table, giving her the eye. "Right! He even got me groceries and put them away. Then, he fixed my shower and the front door. He's coming back to fix the light in the kitchen. We even went to the store and he got me a new shower head, taught me about tools and stuff."

"Wait. Not only did you throw kitty cat, but he cooked, filled your fridge, *and* started fixing the bathroom that's been messed up since you moved in? Along with fixing the door handle you fucked up because you fell?"

"I thought I was locked out and was trying to catch the door. Girl, you know this! Anyways his sexy toolbox and change of clothes were in the car." I shook my head. "I really like him, and I love and hate it."

"Well, enjoy the ride. Just know that this is one time. He needs to show up consistently, too." We ordered our food and drinks, and caught up on work, Shai's experimental recipes and her recent escapades. Then, just as the food was placed in front of us, my phone dinged with a text.

Vernon: I'm missing you, want to meet up with me and some friends in an hour? My treat

"WANT TO MEET MR. HANDY MAN IN PERSON?"

She scoffed and then moaned as she took a bite out of her croissant. "Yea I'll go for a little bit. I need to look him in the eye to see if he's just love bombing you."

I really fucking hoped he wasn't.

Me: I'm with Shai, can she come too? Our friends hanging out

Vernon: Of course sweetheart, see you soon

GOOD, SHAI CAN SCOPE HIM OUT JUST IN CASE I'M TOO DICK BLIND TO see. I was even more giddy, quickly finishing my food.

"You want some cake?" Shai asked. "I'm not leaving here without a lemon slice, and you love to ask for some of mine. I ain't sharing."

"Yes, I want a slice. It's so moist."

I knew it couldn't afford brunch, but I could pretend to open my wallet. I opened it for show and a $100 dollar bill and a sticky note popped out.

My treat.
Vernon

· · ·

"Don't let me get too used to this." I whispered to myself as I put it down to take care of our food.

"What happened to 'I need more clients so I'll die?'"

"Vernon put this in my wallet. He must of did it when I wasn't looking." I showed her the message he left on the sticky note.

Shai gathered her things. "Well let's go meet this 'it's on me' man. Now, I don't want to keep big baller waiting. I'll ride with you."

I texted him when we were outside. It was a cigar lounge in a nice part of town. The parking lot wasn't packed, so we got a good spot close to the door. The parking was free, so that was an even better sign.

He came outside and started walking to my side of the car. He was wearing a green long sleeve shirt with black jeans. His bearded smile could be seen from a mile away. Even from him being far, I could see the silhouette of his abs under his shirt. I wonder if he was free after for some more 'fun time' after our meet up. I thought all men were the same with immaturity or waiting to put actions behind his words, but he's been so intentional so far.

Please don't mess up.

I smiled up at him as he helped me out with an extended hand. "Long time no see sweetheart".

"Hey, Vernon." We quickly hugged when I exited the car, and he kissed my cheek.

More PDA. Mmm, love it .

Then he went around the car and opened Lashai's door. "Hey, I'm Vernon. I'm glad to meet you, Lashai!" He helped her out, and Lashai wore a look of surprise on her face.

"Not helping me out of the car, too! Alright then!"

I rolled my eyes as he chuckled.

When we walked inside, I thought it would be close to a club, but it was a true lounge. Some people were dancing, others were at the bar, and some sat in chairs in front of the TV watching basketball. There was a smoking section and a non-smoking section in the far corner. He took us over to his two friends and we shook their hands.

"These are my friends Elbert and Roswell." Roswell looked excitedly at Shai, and it made me smile for her. Do they know each other? From the way Shai rolled her eyes, they definitely did.

"Do you want something to drink?" Roswell asked us, with a smile and wink towards Shai.

"Yea I can do a Long Island Iced Tea." I nudged Shai to fix her attitude.

"A Lemon Drop for me."

Roswell ordered for us and paid in cash while they stood up, giving up their seats at the bar for us as our drinks were prepared. Shai looked at Roswell in annoyance, but she wasn't pushing him away, more like egging him on. I acted like I didn't peep. When I tasted my drink, it was good and strong.

I might need to come back here.

Vernon got a cigar, and showed me how to light it. "Have you ever smoked?"

"I have, just not regularly."

He put the cigar down after blowing the smoke away from my face. "I'm sorry, we can sit in the non-smoking section. The air is a little better over there." As Vernon and I moved seats, I watched as Shai scooted down a few more seats with Roswell, watching the basketball game on the TV.

"How long have you and your friends known each other?" I asked him.

He chuckled. " Since grade school. We've all kept in touch. Elbert was in the army for ten years and came back, he needed us as bad as we missed his crazy self. The three of us have partied, traveled, grieved, and celebrated with each other. When Beatrice passed, they were there for me, brought food, took Genesis to school, and made sure we ate. We all look out for each other."

Then a glaze came over his eyes, and he looked as if he was deep in thought. The music faded out of my ears as I observed him. I could see his wheels turning and reflecting on the past. The past I had no part in, but was open to hearing about.

I think I want to be in his future.

"Sorry, I didn't mean to zone out on you. Grief is a funny thing…"

I didn't want to intrude, but while the topic was here, I asked. "What was your favorite thing about her?"

He gave me a look that I couldn't read, like he was deciding on how open he should be with me. I didn't want to force him. I placed my hand on his. "You don't have to answer if you don't want to talk about it. But she was important to you, I can tell. And if you're comfortable, I want to be your listening ear."

He nodded. "One of my favorite things about her would be her routine when she just got her hair permed. That was when she would be the happiest. She always refused to cook on the day it got done because she didn't want sweat or anything to mess it up. So Genesis and I would work together in the kitchen. It was one of the few times we could because if Beatrice was behind the stove we weren't allowed past the threshold. She would just sit on the couch and read or go out with her friends. That's why I wanted to make sure her hair was always done because it was important to her and when it wasn't done, it would make her even more stressed. She rarely wore pants or flats, even when walking around the house." He nodded again looking at the palm of his hands. "Then, when Genesis started going to the salon with her, they both relaxed while I worked on dinner." His eyes were glassy, and he began blinking harder.

I hugged him tight, squeezing my arms around his neck. "Thank you for sharing that with me." He could've said "never mind" or "I don't want to talk about it," but he told me about a really tender memory of his family.

He tried to cough to hide the lump in his throat. "Thank you for listening. I didn't know if you would want to hear about her."

"I won't force you, but I'd like to hear about her anytime you want to talk about her. She was important to you, so I hope one day she'd be important to me, too." I nudged his arm as we continued to talk. I told him about the letter from my mom, showed him a picture of her house, and poked fun at Lashai getting cozy with his friend. He told me me about Genesis, her favorite color and hairstyles, and the one time she brought a boy over and Vernon talked him to death about his future. The guy was only fifteen but still. Time flew, and we laughed until it was dark outside. Every time I looked over at Shai, she was basically in Roswell's lap, laughing. I checked in on her twice and both times she wasn't even drunk. He must be the older guy she's given me minimal details to me about.

"Is the music okay?" Vernon asked in my ear, the smell of mint and whiskey on his breath, while smoke filled the air in front of us.

"Yea I like this DJ and the energy. I'm glad the music isn't so loud that it's shaking the walls. I'm surprised I've never heard of this spot."

"It's a nice little hole in the wall. I'm glad you're enjoying yourself."

I eyed him from bottom to top like he was the last glass of water after a three mile run. "Are you doing anything to enjoy yourself after this?"

He bit his lip. "That's up to you. How quick can you get Shai home?"

I grabbed my keys and began to stand up. "Quickly. She's acting like she might not need one from how cozy she is over there with Roswell. My place or yours?"

"Definitely yours. I'll see you there, sweetheart."

He beat me there, of course. After I unlocked my door, my legs were already wrapped around him. He carried me into my room with his hands full of my ass. He placed me at the foot of the bed and pulled my boots and pants off quickly. He pleased me in all the places I wanted him to and more, making himself unforgettable.

I love that.

9

TISHELLE

It was my last day in the office, with Christmas being a few days away. Being the owner of Sweet Honey Agency, I control my schedule, and I needed a real break. I've been busting my ass for months with minimal success. I've only had 3 clients in the last 6 months. I needed a refresh. I wouldn't be coming back until the New Year unless the building caught on fire. I rent this office space in a coworking area. It only costs $25 a month, and it gives me the essentials: a desk, a lamp, internet, and a whiteboard. Was it the size of a closet? Yes, but it was my work closet. The heat in the building also stopped working a few days ago.

Achoo.

While I was worked on mock materials with a blanket wrapped around my shoulders, I noticed Vernon was calling. I quickly answered, "Hey!"

"Hey, baby, how are you feeling?"

Mmm, I loved how his deep voice sounded on the phone.

"Good, just working on mock materials to send to businesses I found on social media that could benefit from a good revamp. I need clients so bad, but people don't want to work around the holidays."

Achoo.

"Sorry, today is my last day working before Christmas break. How are you?"

"Are you coming down with something?"

"No, no, just cold. I'm good. What are you doing?"

"I just finished a meeting about a big project at work, and thinking about you."

With the way his tongue has been acquainted with me, he's on my mind too. But I can't come off as desperate.

"Oh really? I'm still on your mind?"

"Of course, you're on my mind and my heart right now. I want to do something for you."

I checked the time on my laptop, "I'm headed to lunch soon because I'm *starving*."

"What were you going to get?"

I shrugged to myself. "Probably a salad from the deli downstairs. I need to watch my figure before this gala."

He made a disapproving noise. "Is that what you want for lunch? It doesn't sound like it. Let me order you something. I want you fed good. You don't need to worry about your weight because the dress will fit you, not you trying to fit a dress. Whatchu want to eat, baby?"

I'm already a size 18, but he was right. I've been proud about this little pudge. "I'd love a good bowl of chili. My heat stopped working in my office so I'm freezing down to my toes." I tightened the blanket around my shoulders.

"I'll take care of it, just send me your address baby."

"Really?"

"Yes, let your man take care of you."

I smiled to myself as I texted him my office address. Parts of it were open to the public, but only people with office reservations could make it past the door. "I will. I'm sending it to you now."

45 MINUTES LATER, THERE WAS A KNOCK AT THE DOOR FROM THE FRONT desk person, Cheryl. "Tishelle, were you expecting a delivery?"

I opened the door to her pulling a cart behind her. My phone rang with a video call from Vernon. I answered and propped my phone up.

"Cheryl, why do you have a whole cart? It's just supposed to be chili." I looked at screen to see him smiling like the Cheshire Cat. "Bae, I only asked for lunch, why is there a whole cart?"

She unloaded a space heater, an insulated 'hot cold bag', a 6 pack of Oreos, and a bouquet of bright, vibrant purple viola flowers. My jaw dropped as I accepted the arrangement and placed them on my desk.

"Ooo I can't wait to bring these home! Thank you!" I smelled the food while zipping open the bag.

"You're welcome baby, I'm glad everything made your day."

I started unboxing the heater and quickly plugged it in. I could feel the heat on my feet as it quickly filled the small room. While chili warmed my spirit and the blanket wrapped around me, I forgot Vernon was on the phone.

He was sitting quietly, typing on his computer occasionally glancing at me from the top of his glasses. If people couldn't look into my office, I'd flash him or open this Oreo and lick the center, but that might not be the best way to say thank you in public. "Do you have a dress for the gala yet?" he asked me.

"No, I don't think I can get it for a few days. I have a payment depositing soon." I didn't. I'd been living off credit cards and savings. But he didn't need to know that.

"What are you doing now? I'm taking you to buy it."

I looked at my watch. "I was going to do some cold calls until 4."

"Then let's meet at the mall at 5 so I can get you this dress. Our colors need to match anyway. Okay, sweetheart?"

"Yes, sir," I chuckled to myself. We got off the phone and the rest of the work day flew by since I knew I was seeing him in a matter of hours.

❄

LIKE HE SAID, HE WAS THERE EARLY. THE MALL WASN'T PACKED, AND I just hoped they had something in my size that didn't look like a glittery ballon. We looked together through the racks, I didn't think he'd want to be by me. "My tie is champayne so as long as it's close, it'll be fine."

"Who's hosting this event again?"

"The mayor himself."

My eyes widened. How was he able to get a ticket, let alone for the both of us? "When you say you work for the city, what exactly do you do?"

He froze with his hand on the rack, almost like he was surprised I asked. "I'm the Vice President of Water Management Services. You could also call me the Commissioner of the Department of Watershed Management, or the DWM."

I blinked twice. "Vice President? Commissioner? That's not the 'just a city worker putting down pipes' attitude you had at the event."

He wrapped his arm around my waist and pulled me close, "I don't share it most of the time. Sometimes people will treat you different, and I didn't want to be."

I had a top city executive between my legs and he didn't want to tell me? No wonder why he won't let me take out my wallet, he was definitely making 6 figures, if not more. After trying on 4 different dresses, I went with the one that was an open-leg ballroom gown that accentuated my breasts. The look in his eyes when he saw it on me solidified the choice.

Vernon paid for the dress, shoes, diamond earrings and a thick black shawl, carrying them for me to my car. He loaded the car perfectly then opened the door for me on the driver's side.

"Let me cook you dinner tonight to say thank you. You've cooked for me already." I needed to show him how grateful I was in ways other than bending over or having my knees at a 90 degree angle, even though I'm more than open to do that again.

He smiled wide, lowering his glasses. "What time you need me, and what do I need to bring?"

"8. And bring your overnight stuff, cause you ain't leaving."

"Yes, ma'am. I love the sound of that, baby." He bent down and wrapped me in a kiss that lifted me off my feet. I didn't know kissing someone could make you breathless. Our tongues were entwined. I had to force my legs down so they wouldn't be wrapped around his waist. When he placed me back down, I was dizzy.

"I'll see you tonight."

"See you tonight," I said with a shy smile. My backseat was packed with the ensemble he bought me. Now the question was: what was I going to cook to not only impress him, but fill him to the point that he's licking his fingers and me?

MY DOOR BELL RANG AT 7:45. I PEEPED THROUGH THE HOLE AND SAW Vernon was standing there with a bag in one hand and a bottle of white wine in the other. I looked down at my yoga pants and sports bra. He could see me like this. Hell, he's seen me naked plenty of times now. I opened the door.

"Good evening," I said with a warm smile as the cold wind snuck in.

He stepped inside, the cold air creeping up my chest. "Hey, baby," he said before lightly kissing my lips. "I brought wine, I wanted to contribute something."

I accepted it as he followed me into the kitchen to put it in the fridge. "Thank you. Dinner should be ready shortly. I want the cabbage to have more time to simmer."

Vernon deeply inhaled as I pulled the smothered pork chops out the oven. I rubbed my ass on him as he stood behind me, then placed the food on the stove as we smelled the pan together.

"Baby cakes, this smells delicious." The rice and cabbage were warming on the stove, now we can eat. I took out the fresh, steamy cornbread next, spreading honey on it with a brush as he groaned behind me caressing my thighs and rocking side to side. "I didn't know you could cook like this baby. I can't wait to try it."

"You see me cooking a meal like this for you? You know I like you, right?"

He kissed my forehead. "I really like you, too. I hope I haven't been a bother always coming over."

"No! Of course not! I like hosting you. You're the reason my teeth weren't chattering for the rest of the day. Now go wash your hands so you can sit at the table. I'll fix your plate." He walked back to the bathroom in anticipation. I was going to wait for him to come back before I made his plate, but he was taking longer than I thought. I went back and saw the lights on with the door open.

"Is everything okay, babe?" I called.

"Yea, yea!"

I heard something clang so I walked back faster. His hand was screwing the stopper back on. "Your water was flowing out slow, so I pulled out your stopper. It just needed a quick clean."

"So you want to fix something every time you come over?"

He began washing his hands again. "If it needs to be, yea. Baby, let me tell you something: there's a difference between being the man of the house, and a man in the house. A man being in the house, is just there. He doesn't do nothin'. Now a man of the house, takes care of it. You can tell when a man is there. When you have a problem, I fix it, point blank. No excuses. When I walk into your place, I'm the man here and I always want to make sure you feel my presence. So, if that means I take a few minutes to make sure you don't worry I'll do that for ya."

He lathered the soap in his hands without breaking eye contact.

"A man doesn't wait when something needs to get done. You did hard work making this meal so I wanted to take a little extra to fix something you may or may not notice, but makes your life easier." He wiped his hands with a paper towel as the water quickly went down the drain. "Ready?"

A man of the house. I like the sound of that.

"Yea let me fix your plate." I smiled as I walked back to the kitchen with a skip in my step.

A younger guy may not have even noticed-or even if he did notice, not done a damn thing about it. I was nervous about cooking a spread for Vernon, but he keeps showing me that he'll put action behind his words. I like him and I think he likes me too. As he sat down at the table, I put a little bit of everything on his plate and gave him two pieces of cornbread with extra gravy over his rice. From how he looked, he might get some more.

I showed him the plate. "Does this look good? You want anything else on here?"

"No, ma'am. I was going to ask for two pieces of cornbread, but you did that already, sweetness."

As I placed his plate down in front of him, he stood up. "Why are you standing up? I can get our drinks."

"No, you sit down while I fix your plate and bring out the drinks. It won't take me long."

I sat down, still surprised again as he brought my plate and wine glasses. "The wine isn't cold yet. Is that okay, or do you want ice?"

"I'll have a few pieces of ice."

He brought everything, sitting comfortably in his chair before extending his hands for mine. He prayed over the food and we couldn't wait to devour it. We didn't talk much as we ate. I asked how Genesis was doing, and he said well even though he was upset she didn't want to spend Christmas with him. I sympathized and encouraged him to keep talking to her, and he agreed. Christmas was one of the tough holidays for her.

When we finished, he washed the dishes and sat on the couch with me, watching a romantic comedy with a blanket draped over us. I can't explain the calmness I get from laying my head on Vernon. I didn't know I dozed off to sleep until I felt him pick me up, walk me to the room, and lay me in the bed. I sleepily put on my bonnet as he joined me in bed. His arms around me wrapped in a hug just made everything seem okay. I wasn't short on clients, or only had 6 months left on my apartment lease with no backup plan, barely being able to pay the $2300 rent.

He's here with me. He'll take care of me.

❋

HE LEFT THE NEXT AFTERNOON AFTER HE CAME WITH ME TO GET MY nails done and paid, of course. When we got back to my place, he fixed a loose outlet that got my lamp to work. I thought it couldn't be fixed, so I didn't even submit that one to the office. Without feeling my head on his chest or hearing him around the place with his loud toolbox, being in my apartment was starting to feel lonely. I can't explain how excited I got hearing his warm scruffy voice greet me in the morning. Just as I was about to call him to come back, I saw my mom calling and I immediately sat up and answered.

"Mom! You called!"

I could hear rain behind her. "Yes! How are you, sweetheart? I'm sorry I won't be back for Christmas this year."

"It's okay I figured that. What have you been up to?"

She talked about trying a stew her friend made and loving it, another American with dual citizenship, and the cat that lived on her front porch.

"I have to mail you another picture, but she hates the camera. You never let me talk this much unless you have something to hide. What's going on, honey pie?"

"Me? Oh, I've met someone, too... We went on a few dates. He's super intentional and funny, in a corny way. I'm actually in the Christmas spirit. I like listening to him. I hope I get to meet his daughter, but it might be too early."

"How old is she and how old is he?"

"He's forty-seven and she's twenty-two."

My mom made her thinking grunt noise. "An older man? Hmm, that would work for you. But older doesn't always mean more mature, so pay attention to the little things, okay?"

The little things? I sat and thought about it. Every time we've been together, he has paid, fed me, or fixed something.

"I think he's doing that the best. He even fixed the door knob."

She gasped, "He was able to? Wow, I'm impressed. You've been slamming that door for months. I thought you'd throw your shoulder out one day."

I laughed. "I know! I really like him and I think you will, too, mom. It's been a few weeks, but he has me in another world. I haven't had hope in a man like this in awhile. He even randomly puts money in my purse with a little note."

"Good, because a wet cat and a dry purse don't go together."

I roared in laughter. "I'm not going there with you."

"There's a reason my mama told me that, too."

We talked for another hour before getting off the phone. I rarely had to use my purse around him, so that made me feel better about his ability to provide for me and our possible future together. I see it. I do want us to have a future in any way I get if he doesn't want to remarry. But he's mine, and I'm his.

My Christmas tie cutie.

10

TISHELLE

I put on the long champagne dress Vernon bought me. It had spaghetti straps, an open leg, and a heart-shaped silk bodice with a corset that snatched my girls to the heavens. I wrapped the black fur lined shawl around my shoulders so I wouldn't be cold. My hair was blown out into a natural bob, and my black heels paired perfectly with the look. I put on my diamond earrings, then brushed my neck and chest.

"I wish I had a necklace to match." I normally wore gold, but silver would match the earrings.

My face was beat, my purse was packed. It was time for one of the most exclusive holiday parties in Atlanta. I feel like Vernon would've kept his VP commissioner job a secret if I never asked about it. I hope he didn't think I would use him. I would've kept hanging out with him if he was a boss or a blue collar worker.

After dropping the car off to the valet, we walked up to the mansion. There was a walking path lined with Evergreens decorated in warm yellow Christmas lights and glass ornaments.

"Honey?"

I looked at him. He entwined his fingers with mine and we stepped to the side, surrounded by a cool breeze and warm pine scented ambiance. This moment already felt like one of the best dates we have ever been on. I gave him a waiting look as he held my hands, admiring my face as he held them and lighting rubbing his thumbs against my palms.

"Tishelle, you are one of the nicest, caring, and hard working women I know. From simple conversation, my feelings for you are more than anything I have felt in years. I want you to be mine. I want us to be together with no question of commitment."

He went into his jacket pocket and brought out a long slim black box. He opened the felt box and I could see clearly, a silver necklace with a diamond encrusted T at the end. It was simple, but the diamonds sparkled singing, "All I want for Christmas is youuu."

"Tishelle, will you give me a chance this Christmas to be your man?"

My stomach turned in excitement. He put so much thought into everything we've done together. There is no doubt in my answer. How did he remember something I mentioned in passing weeks ago? I've always wanted a necklace like this.

"Baby, in my mind, we were already together, so I'm glad it didn't take you long to make us official. Will you put this on me?"

Vernon chuckled as he took the necklace out of the box and put it on me. I was so giddy, I couldn't hide my grin even if my mouth was duct taped shut. Now I can introduce Vernon as my *boyfriend,* with an almost Christmas anniversary. Once the necklace was secured, I wrapped my arms around his shoulder for a hug.

My man, my man, my man!

The inside of the home was astonishing. The hors d'oeuvres and flutes were refilled before you could turn around. There were multiple conversations happening around us. Then, a woman with brunette hair tied into a low bun, walked up to Vernon and shook his hand. "Lovely to see you here! And who is this lovely lady?"

I extended my hand and replied, "I'm Tishelle."

She shook it firmly. "Nice to meet you. Vernon and I have worked together for at least the past fifteen years. I'm so glad you both could make it."

He put his arm around my waist. "Yes, it's good to see you too, Laurie-Ann. Is your husband here? I haven't seen him since last year."

She rolled her eyes with a smile, "Probably chatting near a plate, bless his heart. What do you do, Michelle?"

Before I take an inhaled breath to respond.

"Her name is Tishelle, with a T." His hand squeezed my hip.

The woman looked shocked. "Oh gosh I'm sorry Tishelle. Guilty as charged, this is my fourth glass."

Damn, we just walked in. "I'm a marketing agent for my own company, Sweet Honey Agency."

Laurie-Ann's eyebrows raised, "Oh! My friend needs one really bad. His computer is fifteen years old and he still thinks he can make his own advertisements. In the New Year I'll get your information from Vernon. I hope to see you all around. I'll see you all later. Enjoy the party!"

Then she walked away. We just walked in and she was on her fourth glass-she's here to party. There was a live band singing popular Christmas songs that could be heard on the main floor. From the back windows, you could see the lit Christmas trees throughout the large property.

"Baby I'm going to get us some drinks."

I nodded, "That's fine."

He kissed my cheek before walking away.

As I was listening to the band from afar, a hush fell over the room in a quiet excitement as I looked around. Around the corner came Vernon and the Mayor of Atlanta himself with a small grin.

"You are the Tishelle I've been hearing about? I'm excited to meet you." He shook my hand as I got star struck.

"It's nice to meet you too, sir." Do I even say sir? I awkwardly chuckled to myself. "How long have you two known each other?"

Vernon gave him a knowing look. "Go ahead and tell her. I haven't yet."

"We're fraternity brothers, actually. He's my big brother," he pushed Vernon mockingly on the chest. "We've been cool ever since. Trust and believe, you have a hard working man right here. I had to convince him to apply to the job with the city. He was the president of facilities management and I knew he'd be great for the city of Atlanta. Did you know he's managing a 4 billion dollar project to redo our water infrastructure?"

A surprised looked took over my face as Vernon looked bashful. "Wow, I didn't know. I'm glad that you both have stayed close through the years."

"Yes indeed," he patted Vernon's shoulders with an *I'm proud of you* look. "It's Christmas and you didn't want to bring out your crimson jacket?

Vernon rolled his eyes, "I don't have to wear it all the time. I'll be wearing crimson and cream for the rest of my life." They laughed together as I chuckled.

The whole night, Vernon introduced me as his girlfriend. It made me feel special and seen, especially as we met congressmen, lawyers, local business owners, and more. I wish I brought business cards. Anytime it looked like a M was rolling off someone's lips when saying my name, Vernon corrected them politely. We even danced on the dance floor with the band. The way he looked at me with his hand rested on my back, I was ready to go and have more fun at home.

My feet were hurting and I didn't bring a back up pair of shoes. Before Vernon went to the valet, he handed me a pair of black slip-on shoes.

"How did you know my shoe size? These have been in your pocket the whole night?"

He nodded and he got on his knees, unclamping my shoes and putting the slip-ons on. "Didn't I already tell you that I don't want you worried about anything around me? You're mine, and I got you, okay?"

I don't know if it was because he was on his knees tending to me, or how he gently massaged my feet before slipping the shoe on.

"I'm headed to the valet. Just sit here and wait for me."

"Yes daddy."

He smiled wide as he walked out to the stand. He got the truck from the valet, and it was toasty warm by the time I got inside. His hand rested on mine as he drove, the lights of the city passing by as we rode down Interstate 400.

Back at my apartment, we quickly got out of our clothes. I removed my make up before we showered together and got in the bed. He brought an overnight bag with his towel, body wash and change of clothes. He easily slipped into the covers behind me, and wrapped his arm around my body as he tried to scoot closer to me. I looked on the nightstand at my new necklace.

I got a boyfriend as a pre-Christmas gift.

Now what can I give him?

11

TISHELLE

When I opened my eyes, I could feel Vernon beside me. As my vision started to clear, I saw a book in one hand and the other scribbling in a notebook. I tried to not make any noise so I could watch him study. He looked from his glasses to his notebook, nodding in understanding.

I smiled with a groan and stretched. "Good mornin'."

He put his pen down and slowly bent down to kiss my nose then my lips. "Good morning beautiful. How did you sleep?"

I stretched again, cracking my back. "Amazing actually. What are you reading?"

He turned the cover towards me. The Holy Bible. "I see you in the word first thing in the morning."

He nodded. "I do it every morning, whether you see me or not. He's the most important thing, next to my family. Have you ever been to church?"

"I have. I grew up going, but haven't been in awhile. I'd be open to going to a service with you either way."

He smiled. "I'm glad to hear that. I didn't want to force you. Any plans for today?"

I rubbed my eyes as I sat up, bringing my blanket around my neck to cover myself from the coolness in the room. "Shai's dinner is tonight but that's it. What about you?"

"I was actually going to invite you somewhere if you wanted to go with me. I reserved a cabin in Blue Ridge. Genesis is still wanting to spend the holiday with friends instead of coming home. Would you want to spend Christmas with me? I have it reserved until January 2nd, so maybe we can be together the whole week. It would be a great way to relax before the New Year."

A week-long cabin stay on Christmas with a sexy man I don't want to spend an hour away from? Yes please!

"Yes, I would love to! That fits my schedule perfectly because I don't go back to work until the Monday after. When do we leave?"

"We'll need to be on the road by two to pass traffic. It's about two and a half hours away." He started to get out of the bed. "I'm going to pick up some groceries, grab my suitcases, then come back and pick you up."

Oh snap, that means I have to pack. Like really pack. Shai is going to beat my ass for canceling at the last minute when all the food is probably made. "Shai is going to kill me, but I'm going to start packing. This is a fun, last minute surprise."

He pulled out his phone, typed something, then my phone dinged.

My Boyfriend: *Sent $500*

"SEND IT TO HER AS A CHRISTMAS GIFT FROM ME... AND AN APOLOGY for taking you away."

I chuckled, "Oh this will make the news sweeter I'm sure. I don't even know what to pack. I haven't had a real vacation in... forever. I've been hunting down clients so much I haven't even thought about taking days off. Will it snow?"

"It's supposed to, so be sure to bring some warm clothes and a bathing suit for the hot tub if we have time." He eyed me up and down. "Besides that, you wouldn't need much clothes, baby. I'm looking at your purest beauty right here."

I leaned in and lightly kissed him. "Thank you." As he went to the bathroom my phone dinged again. He sent me $700.

"Well, looks like I can afford his Christmas gift now," I said to myself with a laugh. I'll need this to survive Lashai cursing me out.

"SO YOUR BALD HEADED ASS CALLED ME TO CANCEL? OVER SOME DICK? We do this every year! I've been cooking since last night to make sure we had enough. Come on, girl."

My jaw dropped as I looked at the screen. "Damn, I said I was sorry. I didn't know! But why I gotta be bald headed? You didn't even let me finish, I have some news to share, too."

Her hand paused over the stove and slowly turned towards me. "If he proposed and you said yes without seeing where he lays his head, you are stupider than I thought. Go ahead, what do you need to tell me?"

I pursed my lips, not taking offense because it was true, just unrelated. I know Shai was hurt about me not coming since she's hosted this dinner every Christmas Eve for the past five years. I used to offer to come over and help, but I confused salt for sugar one time and I was banned from her kitchen. It happened almost 10 years ago and she still reminds me every now and then.

"Vernon didn't propose, he just officially asked me out right before the gala. It was sweet with him introducing me to everyone. I even met the mayor and a few other socialites."

Shai made a face like she didn't care. "That's why your ass is deserting me. Ight then. I guess I'll allow it."

I took this time to pause packing and send the $500. She squinted when it popped up on her phone. "The hell?"

"This is from Vernon as a Christmas gift and apology. I still got your gift and will bring it over in a few hours. Is that okay?"

"I guess so. I'll miss you and will throw this food out."

I frantically shook my head. "No! Girl, just put it in the freezer for me. I'll take it all." She could at least save me enough for two plates. Shai always overcooked anyway. I would've invited Vernon if he didn't have this surprise.

Shai grumbled, "Now what are you packing since you want to go and have sexy Christmas time with your new boyfriend? What happened to the black bra and thong combo?"

I nodded digging into my drawers then holding it up. It was a mesh bralette and thong set that I forgot I even owned.

"I forgot I even had this. See? You do still like me."

"Uh huh, Vernon's gift helped me not curse you out even more. Even though you're leaving me for some dick."

Oh, let me remind my girl of something. "Like how you were ducked off at the lounge? Don't think I forgot about you getting all cozied up. He's the one you've been talking about sparingly, right? Silver fox? You didn't know he knew Vernon. This is a small city."

Shai rolled her eyes. "It was our first time on a 'real' date. That's why he was so excited. I wasn't expecting to have fun. I thought I was going to get a free drink then tip toe out. Sike! We rode together and I didn't want to pay for an Uber. We haven't hung out since, though, mainly because I canceled." She shrugged. "We'll see what happens."

I made a face at her. "Someone once told me to get outside of my comfort zone with dating."

She rolled her eyes again. "Okay? And someone else put salt in some damn cupcakes."

"Let that go! It was an accident!"

We laughed hard while I finished collecting my toiletries and checking everything around the house. When I went over to drop off her gift, she gave me mine as well and said I could open it tomorrow. I hugged and squeezed her so tight. I was looking forward to our yearly get together of the best food I could have in my life. Sometimes I could just imagine her cookbook with her standing in front of her pie with a wide trusting smile.

12

——————

TISHELLE

As Vernon and I rode further north, I could feel it getting colder and colder, but the heat blowing on my face in Vernon's truck was comfy. Not only were the windows cold but the snow started to fall from the sky. It wasn't thick enough to stick though. I dreamily looked out the window to the sound of Toni Braxton's voice on the radio. The trees were thick and lush

"So what do you like sweetheart?"

I arched my eyebrow. "Like what? Food? I saw enough groceries in the back to feed a family. I think we have enough for the week."

He chuckled. "No, sexually. Have you been pleased with everything we've been doing?"

Oh, that's what he meant. "Yes I have. I think you're romantic, great at foreplay, give the best massages, and that little flick of your tongue you did on my clit... mmm, that'll have me jacking you off on the way there." I chuckled to myself as he made an approving face, still paying attention to the road. "All I could maybe want more of is you holding me tighter and squeezing me. I love the caresses, just mixing them in and smack my ass more. Those would be my only notes. What about you? Am I pleasing you?"

"Sweetie, you've been pleasing me in ways I can't describe. You've got a slice of heaven in you, baby. You make my knees weak when I look into your eyes."

I bashfully looked away. "I feel the same too." I'm really spending Christmas with him. I was hoping Genesis would change her mind, I really wanted to meet her, but at least this will be romantic. Though he has not failed in that department yet.

"Is there anything new you want to try or are curious about?" I could see his hand fidgeting on the wheel, waiting for my response.

"You won't think I'm weird?" My brain has... *pondered* some ideas, but he's not about to judge what I want to try.

"Depending on the answer, I'll be truthful with my response."

I exhaled, if he's not into this then it might change the energy for the rest of this vacation. I'll just blurt it out.

"I wouldn't be mad with food being licked off me or licking it off you. Maybe chocolate?"

He's nodding, maybe that's not a bad sign.

"Even though you're delicious enough by yourself, I would lick anything off your sexy body."

I smiled to myself, "I'm looking forward to it."

After driving for a total of 3 hours, we pulled into a single level log cabin. The driveway was clear, next to a sitting area by a firepit that looked charming. The perfect setting for a Christmas card Kodak moment.

Vernon quickly opened his door. "Can you wait in here while I unload everything? I want to make sure the heat is on."

"Of course, I'll be here."

He grabbed a couple of his bags and one of mine in the back and went inside. I started playing with a social media post template when the car door suddenly opened to Vernon standing there holding in a smile.

"Did you do something? I zoned out working so I don't know how much time just passed."

He looked confused, "Do something? No, I just went inside to drop all the bags off baby. Ready to go inside?"

I gave him a side eye as I stepped out, pulling my silk lined beanie lower on my head to avoid the chill. He held my hand as we walked up the driveway to the wreath-decorated front door. He opened the door and I walked into the cozy cabin. The Christmas tree in the corner was decorated in beautiful red and green lights with gifts under it; the fireplace was roaring and dim moody lights shined were on in the living room. There was a comfy couch with Christmas pillows by the tree, but the music playing was the cherry on top. Slow R&B played in the background. The kitchen had ribbons on the cabinet doors with a gas stove.

"Santa came already?"

"He did, but I think he'll come back if you ask nicely."

I laughed as I leaned into him, lightly kissing his lips as his hands went up my back. "Care to give me a tour?" I whispered against his lips.

He tightly gripped my ass, then smacked it. "I know my way around here already," he said before kissing me. "Because it's mine."

I lifted my leg, aching to feel closer to him. He quickly lifted me up, not breaking the kiss as he laid me on the couch, gently placing me on the pillows as he got on top. The smell of pine and cinnamon surrounded us as I pulled off his shirt, caressing his chest up to his neck, our lips never disconnecting. This felt even closer than before with barely any air or space between us until we needed to undress. Was it the romance of the cabin or the fact that I don't want to spend a day without him anymore?

We moved into our bedroom, pine and quilts welcoming us as we joined our bodies together again and again. His fingers were running through my hair, nails digging into my sides, his lips never leaving mine as he stroked. Then he flipped me on my stomach, gripping and holding me open as he slid in and out over and over again. He smacked and squeezed my ass leaving his mark. I can't wait to do this for the whole week.

AFTER WE FINISHED AND TOOK A SHOWER, I NOTICED A PAIR OF GREEN satin pajamas and other Christmas themed lounge wear next to it.

Some sets were shorts and some were pants. I dried off, lotioned my body, then put on a shorts set before going back to the kitchen. Vernon was wearing the pants and nothing else while mixing together some batter. "Would you be in the mood for some Cookies and Cream cookies?"

I turned my head to the side and crossed my arms. "Let me get this straight. You made sure everything was romantic before I walked in, bought us matching pajamas, and now you're making cookies with no shirt. You want me to pounce on you, huh?"

He shrugged with a small smile, "I want this to be special for us, so you know how special you are to me. Come here."

I slowly walked over, swinging my arms. He grabbed my hand and pulled me into him, lightly kissing my lips and my nose.

"Now, do you want to help with these cookies or not?"

I turned facing the counter, my back firmly pressed against his chest as his beard tickled my shoulder. "What can I do?"

He reached his arms around me, grabbing the dough, surrounding me with his warm scent. "We can form them into balls like this." He mended and patted the dough, placing them on the sheet. I followed along, us playfully bumping into each other as he stayed behind me.

"Any thoughts on dinner?" I asked as I placed the last cookie on the sheet.

"Lasagna soup? It has to simmer and can keep us warm." He grabbed the sheet and placed it in the preheated oven.

"That does sound good." I hummed. "While you start that, I'll make a pitcher of Christmas cocktails to go with it so we won't have to worry about drinks for the week."

He stepped from behind me to in front of the stove and I already missed him. "You have to go all the way over there?"

He came back and kissed my neck. "We have to eat baby. If I keep staying close to you we'll be starving and drained." Vernon turned back to the stove, boiling the lasagna and getting it started. I just watched his back as he moved around the seasonings and pots. After a few minutes he looked over his shoulder at me.

"Now you're staring?"

I nodded, biting my lip as I looked at his ass, "I am. I like our color coordination. What will we wear tomorrow?"

"If it's up to me, nothing. You're the gift I want under the tree." He looked at me like he could drink me in one gulp.

"See, when you talk to me like that it makes me want to bend over. Hand me the pitcher, please."

He laughed as we searched the cabinets and found a plastic one. Were the Christmas cocktails just cranberry mimosas? Yes. But they were still delicious. It didn't take me long to make, and the cookies were done quicker than we thought, too. When the timer on Vernon's phone dinged, I pulled them out of the oven and the sweet decadent smell of chocolate filled the kitchen. Vernon moved to stand right behind me, caressing my back as I purposefully scooted back into him more.

"Alright now, you about to start something. Makes me think of something you wanted to try."

He playfully poured a drop of chocolate syrup onto his finger, then swiped it on my neck. "As your wish," he whispered before giving me a painfully slow lick as I groaned. "You still taste better."

I got some syrup and tapped it on his lips before kissing him, licking it off of his lips. Then he pushed himself against me on the counter, kissing me deeper and deeper.

"Lean your head back," He demanded.

I leaned my head back as he eased my shirt over my head, then he squirted a small line of chocolate between my breast. But instead of licking it off immediately, he swirled it on my nipples, across my breast. Then licked and kissed the remaining chocolate as I groaned.

"Baby," he moaned as the ache grew in my chest. Then started sucking both of my nipples as I started to squirm. I grabbed the back of his head, pushing my pelvis onto him as he lightly nibbled.

"Get under the tree," I demanded.

He laid on the rug in front of the tree. His head was on the floor as I licked my lips and joined him on the floor with the chocolate syrup in my hand. After he pulled off his pants, I poured a line of dark sweetness from the top to the bottom of his dick. It was so pretty and thick, staring up at me. Ready and waiting for me. I licked him from base to tip, sucking him clean while I rubbed up the front of his chest, brushing his nipples. Hearing him groan and moan just made me go faster and faster and deeper in my throat.

"Baby, I'm about to -."

I wasn't moving as the sweet heat eased down my throat and he breathed shakily. "I've always wanted to do that." I said with a smile.

He grunted as he sat up, still at full attention. "Glad we could help." I laughed as we both leaned against the couch to stand back up.

"Look here, I'm starting to get sore from everything we've been doing."

Now he was laughing harder. We have been having a lot of sex without protection in sight. I mean, he's been pulling out but you never know. When Vernon put his pajama pants back on, the lasagna soup was ready. He fixed our bowls and cocktails then brought them to the couch. We watched a typical Christmas movie where you know how it ends, but it was still nice. Vernon was laughing harder than I was at certain parts but it was cute.

After we finished and cuddled under the blanket for another hour, Vernon stood up from the couch with a stretch. "I'm going to take a shower. Just come in when you're ready in 20 minutes or so."

I nodded, "That's specific".

He headed back into the bedroom, closing the door behind him. After 30 minutes, I went back into the room 'as I was told.' Vernon was nowhere to be found as I started undressing before going into the bathroom. As soon as I walked in I noticed the shower had changed. Eucalyptus was now hanging from the shower head and a couple of candles around the sink were now burning. It felt warm and romantic. I looked outside the door to see if this was just for me. When I closed the door, I saw a Christmas card with Santa Claus in his sleigh and reindeer waving. I chuckled to myself, opening it and reading:

Enjoy this shower spa!
You deserve time to rest and relax too
Your boyfriend, Vernon

I LOOKED AROUND ADMIRING THE DARK, CALM AMBIANCE IN THE ROOM. My shoulders instantly relaxed as I rolled my neck. When I put my bonnet on and got in the shower I started crying. Was it because of happiness? Or sadness? He's being so nice to me and keeps one upping himself. Is there a catch I'm missing, because I haven't been this happy in a long time.

When I stepped out, my towel was ready for me as I dried off. In the bedroom Vernon was sitting reading a book when he looked up at me. "Hey, how was the shower? Relaxing?"

"Yes, it was. Thank you for the moment. Would you believe I actually cried?"

"Come here," he opened his arms for me. "Why did you cry?"

I grabbed one of his clean T-shirts, threw it on and got into bed in his arms. "You've just been... really nice. I love how thoughtful you are. You're a great planner and you take care of me so well. I've never had someone prepare so much for me. The cabin, the shower. I just hope this is real, you know?"

Vernon's strong arms surrounded me as I laid on his chest. "You deserve every great thing that happens to you. I know I'm at the tail end of your year, but I have seen you put in work. That's why I like making sure you relax and take time by yourself because you do deserve it." He squeezed me tighter, his soft beard rested on my forehead.

I'm falling in love.

This man is perfect for me. I started rubbing my hand on his length as he looked at me hungrily.

"Do you mind?" I asked.

Vernon bent down kissing me and squeezing me in his arms as I rolled on top of him. Our bottoms quickly discarded as he entered my palace again and again. My hands firmly on his chest, his eyes locked on mine. There was no such thing as time, I just knew I didn't want to stop. We rolled around the bed, our bodies entangled in every way. Our sweat becoming one. He whispered and coached me through his strokes. *You're so beautiful, that's my girl, take it- I know you want it.* I could only whimper and moan yes.

"You have me mesmerized baby I don't want to stop."

"I don't want you to stop. It's yours." I groaned against his lips as he climaxed in me. I didn't run or push him away, instead I held on for more, aching for more of his seed.

Merry Christmas to me.

Christmas Morning

I woke up and rubbed the other side of the bed. Empty. *He's such an early bird.* I rubbed my eyes coming down the stairs, not even remembering moving from our cuddles last night.

"Merry Christmas!" Vernon cheered with open arms, surrounded by gifts in front of the tree.

I yawned and opened my arms, relaxing in the hug turned swinging me around. "Merry Christmas," I said against his chest.

"I can't wait to give you your gifts." He gave me 2 wrapped presents, and I quickly opened them. One was a set of pearl earrings and a necklace; the other was a black designer suit.

"Baby, these are beautiful. Thank you," I said before giving him a kiss. "I'll be right back with your gift!" Goodness, I hope he likes it. I came back out and handed him the green wrapped box. Will it compare to the gifts he got me? No. But I can try. "I haven't seen you wear one of these, so I hope you would like it."

He lifted the top and nodded with a wide grin. "This is beautiful." He turned it over to the engraving... V.C. "You got my initials? I love watches, I just don't get to wear them often. I really like this, baby. You did great."

He walked towards me and kissed my cheek as we sat on the

couch together with my head on his shoulder. I wished my mom were here. I miss her so much.

My phone rang with a photo of me and my mom as the thought crossed my mind. "She's calling!"

I answered the video chat, still sitting on his lap. "Hey Ma."

"Hey baby... ooo, who is this handsome man on the screen?"

"This is my boyfriend."

She made an approving face. "Oh, this is Mr. Vernon. Well, you've made an impression on my daughter. I need to visit and meet you in person."

"Nice to meet you," he said with a charming smile. "I can't wait to hear about your travels."

I gave her a tour of the cabin and showed her my gifts. Then I apologized about why I couldn't mail hers in time and she understood. My gift budget didn't change until I started receiving these gifts.

We waved and ended the call, him holding my legs into his lap. "See, she likes me, too."

I chuckled. "I'm glad, because she didn't have a choice."

The door slamming shut scared me so bad I leapt from the couch as Vernon stood in front of me, with squared shoulders. I looked and saw a young woman in her early 20's with long brown hair wearing a crewneck, thick bubble jacket, sweats and a pair of Uggs with Vernon's eyes. I bet this is -.

"Well, Merry Christmas to you, too, dad! I went by the house to surprise you. Come to find out, you're here in the middle of nowhere. I had to drive through the snow." She glanced at me, then back to Vernon. "So you hired a whore for Christmas?"

My mouth dropped. "Excuse me!"

"Genesis, you need to apologize. Right. Now!" He said as he walked closer to her. "Tishelle is my girlfriend, girlfriend. Now I know this isn't the best way to meet for the first time, but I've been trying to call you all week and every time I tried to talk to you, you were with friends. You need to check yourself."

Genesis' bottom lip quivered. "So, you're forgetting about mom?

You really didn't love her. I wanted to be home for Christmas so I could remember her."

She ran out to her car and he gave me a pained look.

"Go after her, I'm okay."

He squeezed my hand and went out the door behind her. It felt like reality was crashing down.

13

VERNON

I CLOSED THE DOOR BEHIND ME, THE SNOW WAS THICK AROUND THE driveway as I pulled my jacket close to my chest.

"Come back here!" I yelled. Genesis turned around with her car door opened. "We need to talk. How did you even know where I was?"

She rolled her eyes and scoffed as she kept stomping towards her car, the Camry I bought her on her sixteenth birthday.

"Your location is shared with me 24/7, remember? You shared it after I saw that documentary about people decomposing for weeks because nobody noticed they weren't moving or following their usual patterns. I thought it was weird you were hanging out more and at the same apartment complex. But I didn't think anything of it. I *definitely* didn't think you would be out here doing... doing whoever!"

I squared my stance. "Young lady, I'm your father. You don't get to question what I do. Now I understand how this is a lot. But remember, we didn't plan to spend Christmas together. You said you would be with friends. Instead of sitting in the house, hurt, I planned something nice for a woman who is special in my life. My girlfriend. I booked this cabin weeks ago. Now go back inside and apologize to Tishelle. You will act like you have an ounce of sense."

"Girlfriend?" She twisted her neck. "A real girlfriend? I don't believe it. Mom wouldn't -."

"You don't know what your mother would've wanted!" I yelled. Shock spread across her face. "You were too young to understand the conversations she and I had before she passed. Now get your narrow tail back in the house and apologize. Then after you apologize, decide if you want to spend the day here with us or not."

I crossed my arms and looked at her as she gave me sorrowful eyes before she slammed the car door. I remember the first day I met Beatrice when she was a receptionist. I came back every day for a week, asking for her number. The first time she told me no, I said I understood and left. But I still kept coming by, asking how she was doing, bringing her lunch. Then, after two weeks of us getting to know each other, she wrote her phone number on a card and gave it to me. I remember the perfume she was wearing and the smile she had. Her trying to look away but not being able to hide the blush on her cheeks.

Now, so many years later, our daughter shares her mother's eyes and passion. It makes my heart swell that it was Beatrice's hard work through the years of our marriage that brought us here. I'll always be thankful to her for that. That's why when she got sick, I dropped everything. I took a leave from work to go to appointments, tried to manage her hair the best way I could, and filled her prescriptions.

On her last days, I put her lipstick on her because it was most important to her, always. I held her hand as she departed from our world into heaven. I sighed looking away and back at Genesis. Even though I haven't known Tishelle for long, no matter what, her and my daughter need to have a healthy relationship. I'm happy to see Genesis, but she definitely surprised us. I won't tolerate her disrespecting Tishelle, under any circumstance. I gave Genesis a look as she stuffed her keys back into her purse. Then she rolled her eyes back to me.

"Alright, I'll go back in there and apologize. You used to tell me everything."

I ignored her last comment as we walked back inside together. I made it clear that I wanted to see her on Christmas but she gave me excuses every time. Genesis looked at me, then Tishelle with an "*I don't know what you want me to say*" look. As she stood by the front door still.

"Genesis Louise Carpenter, is there something you would like to say to Tishelle?" I lightly pushed Genesis towards her. Why is my child embarrassing me like she's thirteen?

She rolled her eyes, "I'm sorry I called you a whore. You surprised me. I wasn't expecting my dad to have a.... special friend."

"A girlfriend." I corrected.

"A girlfriend," she repeated. "I didn't mean to disrespect you. I was just... caught off guard since I literally didn't know you existed. I would like to stay and hang out. I have missed my dad."

Tishelle looked uncomfortable on the couch before she stood up, wiping her hands on her pants. "I understand the shock. I didn't know about the surprise either. I can just... sit upstairs so you can spend quality time with your dad."

Genesis smiled. "Great!"

"No, not great." I added. "Either we're all together or not."

Genesis rolled her eyes. "Fine. This is my fault, I guess."

Tishelle blew out air and put on a smile. "Well Genesis I have heard a lot about you. I'm looking forward for us spending the day together."

I exhaled too.

I get to have both of my girls together.

14

TISHELLE

After a few hours Vernon followed Genesis out to make sure she made it to the car okay. When he came back inside, he sat on the couch with me, pulling my legs onto his and holding me close as I leaned in for a quick kiss.

"How are you feeling?" I asked him.

He smiled and looked me in the eyes. "I'm glad Genesis stayed and got to know you. It was rough at the start, but that's why some surprises aren't great surprises."

I chuckled, leaning my head on his. "Do you think I made a good impression? I know it was a lot for her."

He gently brushed my face. "Sweetheart, you did. I'm glad my girls finally got to meet."

I blew out more air, leaning against his chest. "It's not that late. What do we do now?"

"How about I get the hot tub started to help us relax?"

"That's why you wanted me to bring a bathing suit?" I asked looking up at him.

He nodded. "It's snowing but the water will keep you warm."

I chuckled. It would relax my joints. I'm so glad Genesis decided to surprise pop up today and not last night. I would've hidden under the bed for what she would've seen us do. I shook my head to myself.

"I'll put on my suit."

Dressed in a robe and my bikini, I peaked through the window and saw Vernon outside turning on the jacuzzi and testing the water. I wish I had a 'V Cam' so I could watch him all day every day. He could've let me go upstairs so he and Genesis could have quality time, but he made a point to include me like he wanted me to be in his life for a while. I could still hear him saying *"My girls finally got to meet"* echoing in my mind.

After a few minutes I came down. Vernon hung my robe and helped me get inside then he followed. We sat in silence, looking at the trees, watching the falling snow. My hair was in a high ponytail so I wasn't too worried about it getting wet.

With his arm wrapped around me, we gazed out into the snow dusted forest. If it wasn't for the rising water I could've fallen asleep. I lifted my head, brushed my thumb on his chin and kissed him. We kissed for what seemed like hours, enjoying the water, the view, and each other's lips.

I never want to leave him.

3 Days Later

It was now December 28th, that weird time after Christmas where it still feels too soon to take down any decorations, but you're still thankful to not be at work. Well, it's not like I have clients, but still. I was working on my laptop on the couch, mindlessly staring at my bank account and the rent that would be due on the 1st . My savings were almost done. Maybe I could sell a few things. I touched the necklace Vernon gave me, too special.

"I can *feel* how hard you're thinking. What are you working on that has you so stressed?"

I turned my laptop towards him. "Just some math that isn't mathing."

He pulled his glasses from his shirt to read the screen then he shook his head. "Can I hold this for a second?"

"It's pretty depressing, but sure." Even if he stole my account information, he wouldn't get much. Probably more debt and depression. He left the room for a few minutes, then reentered, handling my laptop back to me.

I clicked around and saw my rent account portal, "Processing $15,000 payment."

"Excuse me! Did you just pay $15,000 towards my rent? I won't have to pay it for it for the rest of the year."

"I don't like to see you worrying about something I can fix for you baby." He kissed my nose. "Now you can focus on creating mock logos, social media posts, promotion materials, content, or whatever you need creatively."

"You don't know how much you helped me. I was about to sell my couch to make this payment." I squeezed his hand. "I just wish someone would respond back to all my cold calls and inquiries."

He rubbed my palm, "It'll come, baby. Your next assignment is right around the corner. I've been praying for you to receive it, so it's coming right on time."

I squeezed his hand again. Him paying my rent for the rest of the year definitely took some pressure off my chest. Vernon's phone rang and he quickly answered.

"Hey, man, what's hap-... wait what?... Slow down, slow down the ambulance is headed there now? Give me a few hours, I'm out of town... I'm so sorry. Everything will be okay, I'm sure.... I'm heading there right now."

I sat up as he ended the call. "What happened?"

"You remember my friend that you met at the lounge, Elbert? That was his wife, he had a stroke and she's taking him to the hospital. I have to go. I can get you an uber so you can stay here a while."

I got up from the couch with him. "An Uber? I'm going with you. I'm not letting you go by yourself. If you don't want me in the room, I'll sit in the waiting area for however long."

He met my eyes. "You don't have to, you know. You can stay here until the New Year?"

"No. I'm going with you. That's final." I started walking to the bedroom, right to my suitcase to fill it. "I can take care of you, too. I'm driving us there so you can process this and call Genesis. She would want to know, too. You can also get some money back by ending the reservation early."

He stood there frozen and shocked, like he was trying to digest everything but the world was spinning. If anything happened to Lashai, I'd be confused and lost, too.

"Let me take care of you." I eased him into the chair by the bed.

I quickly packed our clothes and groceries, checking every nook and cranny, making sure that I didn't leave even a phone charger behind. As I finished the bags, Vernon packed everything in the car. He still insisted on driving but he called Genesis as we were leaving.

I stayed with him when we made it past admissions, into the elevators, and through the cold hallways. Even though it was the middle of the day, the halls and waiting rooms had just enough people. When we made it to the ICU, he squeezed my hand. "You can wait here or leave if you want."

I shook my head, "I'll wait here, take as much time as you need." I said a silent prayer for Elbert. I didn't talk to him much at the cigar lounge, but he means a lot to me because he means a lot to Vernon.

A movie was playing in the waiting area so I stayed awake, occasionally glancing at the door until Vernon came back out 2 hours later. When I saw him, I smiled and he feigned a smile back at me.

"How was he?" I asked standing up walking out with him.

"He's stable, he hasn't been this bad in a while. He's really going to have to make some changes to his diet. It was weird because I think he knew it was me talking to him, but he couldn't talk back." He quickly wiped his eyes then held my hand. He looked emotionally and physically exhausted.

"You know it's okay to cry right? Especially in front of me?"

He nodded, but looked away. "Yea, I know. I just don't want to right now." I squeezed his hand as we stepped into the elevator.

· · ·

WE SAT IN SILENCE AS HE DROVE ME HOME. WHEN HE PARKED IN A close spot, I asked, "Do you want to come inside? I can fix us some lunch with the leftover groceries."

He shook his head. "I have bothered you enough and you deserve some rest, too. Genesis is probably waiting for me since I told her. I don't want to keep her waiting either. Do you want to go to Watch Night Service with me on New Years Eve? I'm pretty active in my church, and have been a member for over fifteen years. I understand if you don't want to."

"Of course I'd go with you." I've been seeing him read his Bible, pray over our food and my goals. I would love to go with him. "Just let me know if you need anything." I kissed his cheek and got out. He got out with me and gathered my suitcase. When everything was inside, we had a quick goodbye kiss and I watched him leave from the window.

WATCH NIGHT SERVICE WAS A FEW NIGHTS LATER, IT WAS CASUAL, SO I dressed in jeans, black boots, a long sleeve shirt and a coat. When we walked in, he instinctively grabbed my hand. It surprised me this time because I assumed this was the church his family grew up going to. He greeted a few deacons, shaking their hands and introducing me. Everyone seemed excited that I was there and which helped calm the butterflies in my stomach. We got there 20 minutes early and the sanctuary was already filling up.

Genesis came in right at the start of service and sat on the other side of Vernon. I hadn't been to church since I was a kid. I redownloaded the Bible app right before the choir got started so I could take notes. Everything was beautiful, from the songs the choir sang to seeing everyone participate in service. The sermon encouraged everyone to set expectations for God in the New Year and be prepared to take action. Service ended after midnight and I was trying to hide

my yawn. I hoped Vernon and I can come back together this coming
Sunday.

15

TISHELLE

When we made it back to the car after the first Sunday Service in the new year, I saw that Shai texted me.

> Shai Bestie: Sunday brunch? I got a reservation

> Me: Is it cool if bae comes?

> Shai Bestie: Uh huh bring your lil boyfriend whicha

We arrived at the restaurant at the same time and I hugged her tight.

"Girl, you look nice! Where are you coming from?"

"Church." I said it knowing she wouldn't believe me.

She rocked back like she was hit with a bomb. "Church? Like with a preacher and everything?" She looked at Vernon, "You've got my girl back to the Lord? They don't make 'em like you anymore."

Vernon roared with laughter as I tapped her arm. "Hush, let's just sit down and eat."

The server guided us to seats by the window. It was my first time at this restaurant but if Shai chose it, I knew the food was good. Vernon pulled out both of our chairs, mine first, and we reviewed the menu. We ordered and ate our food quickly, Vernon sat quietly as we ate, chiming in every now and then.

"I'm headed to the restroom." He got up from his seat and walked away.

Shai hit my arm, "Quick give me a *real* update of what happened."

"Girl the week at the cabin was... WHEW! The kitchen, under the tree; it was just loving all over. *Then* his daughter, Genesis, randomly showed up unannounced on Christmas Day and caused a whole scene. This child called me a whore and everything. But then she stayed and was halfway pleasant. Then he paid my rent for the rest of my lease. We went to the hospital, then church. It's been crazy."

"That is crazy! He took you over to his house?"

I shook my head. "No, why would he do that?"

Shai scrunched her face. "You realize you've never been over to his house and he spends a bunch of time at yours or rents y'all a place. It's been a month now."

I blinked. I didn't know the point she was trying to make and I looked at her like a lost child.

"I know you failed math because you can't put 2 and 2 together. That man has something in that house. Heck his wife might be there, or something he's keeping you away from. Have you ever thought about why you haven't been over there? Have you even seen any pictures?"

I gasped, he wouldn't do that to me. Everything has just been a... coincidence. Right? *He's not on social media. I've never even seen a picture of Beatrice.*

"Hey honey, I'm back. They brought the check yet?"

"Nope, not yet." I swallowed with a worried face.

Shai is right, I've been playing too innocent and trusting. I've been swept up in this gorgeous, strong man's arms, getting piped down like a house under construction. I didn't even notice, there were so many moving pieces.

We drove home silently as I looked out the window. "Everything okay, baby?"

"Yes, just thinking about service... It made me think alot." Vernon slept over at my place the night of our first date, but he's never invited me over to his. I don't want to bring it up and push him away right now, I might be too emotional. So I just decided to stay quiet, while my mind thought about the worst possible scenarios.

16

VERNON

Since Genesis is going back to school next week, I wanted to take her to Bea's favorite restaurant as a tradition.

As soon as the greeter saw me she cheered, "Oh Vernon! It is so good to see you." We hugged. "I wasn't sure if you were coming by this year."

"It's good to see you too, it's been a while. Genesis will be here shortly, she wanted to drive herself."

"Still keeping the tradition, I was hoping to see you two today. We still keep your booth empty when we can." She walked me to our table. I exhaled at Bea's old seat next to mine as a weight fell onto me. It wasn't sorrow, but acceptance. Seeing Genesis walk in wearing a crewneck with a purse on her shoulder filled me with love. She's grown so much, I don't understand where the time has gone. I remember the first time I held her and kissed her forehead at the hospital while Beatrice's eyes were filled with happy tears. Now, Genesis in her twenties favors her mother, the mother we both lost almost a decade ago.

I was getting choked up, and so was she. When we hugged, I squeezed her for a few moments longer than normal. Where has the little girl that ran circles around my legs gone?

"Hi, Daddy."

"Hey, sweetie."

We sat down as memories began flooding the both of us. Genesis' eyes began to fill, too.

"Dad, do you remember when mom ordered the Calamari and sent it back after finding out it was squid?"

I remembered that day vividly. She wanted to try something new and instantly regretted it when Genesis told her what it really was.

I chuckled. "She was so disgusted. The face she made when she dipped it in mustard like a piece of catfish and took a bite." I chuckled and Genesis roared in laughter.

"You were so embarrassed because of how loud we were laughing at each other. I wish..."

I touched her hand. "I know, baby." I watched as she looked around the seat. "This used to be Mom's favorite place. That was her seat because she said the light hit her better there. No matter where she went, it was like she was a model. Then, she always ordered the clam chowder."

"And never finished it." We said in unison and laughed.

"And you've moved on now with that bi-"

I gave her a warning look. I already told her about her attitude on Christmas, after popping up on grown folks.

"Tishelle, yea. Your new 'girlfriend.'"

I dated women when she was in high school, never the teachers, and she barely cared. Now my current relationship was causing a riff and I don't understand why.

"You didn't care about who I was dating when you were in high school. Why is it so important now?"

"You weren't serious with them," she sighed with crossed arms. "You didn't look at them the same way you look at her... You look at her like you're in love. Like how you looked at mom when y'all would randomly dance in the driveway or if she playfully locked you out and you would sing a random song so off-key she'd pity you." She laughed to herself. "It seems like you moved on and forgot about her."

"I didn't forget her, sweetheart. I'll never meet another woman like Beatrice again. When she got sick... The treatments, her losing hair, the look in her eyes when she was tired of fighting." I put my head down, thinking of the last squeeze she gave my hand when her spirit was on this Earth.

"I knew your mother for over 25 years, before you were even a thought in our mind. During her last days, she said she wanted me to be happy. She didn't want me to feel stuck to her if she was in the grave. Our vows were until death."

I wasn't always the best husband to her; it took watching Genesis grow up to realized how much of her life I really was missing. I was only able to give Beatrice 10 *good* years of marriage when she deserved far more, more from me.

I swiped my eyes quickly. "That's why I'm grateful for Tishelle. She's opened a part of my heart that I thought was broken for good."

I have been more sensitive and open in this new relationship. I thought Beatrice was the only one with the key.

"I understand, Dad."

We reviewed the menu we had memorized for show. I was trying to kill time, too. There had been something I've been wanting to talk to Genesis about for awhile. I just hope she doesn't get angry. When we ordered and the food came, we prayed over the food and began eating quietly.

"You've gone quiet. Something is on your mind," she sighed, "I have a feeling I know what it is."

I met her eyes. "You're right, missy. I have something to tell you. I hope us sitting here brings your mother's spirit here and helps me find the words."

I took a deep breath. "There is something on my mind that may make you angry but I'd rather tell you now then you find out later... I'm selling the house."

Her jaw fell as her eyes widened. "You're what! No, Dad! Do you need money? Maybe I can... Maybe I can work full time. I can take a break from school to help."

My heart broke that she thought she should stop school for me. Money was never an issue.

"That's not it. The house is a lot of upkeep. I don't need four bedrooms anymore. There are boxes just piled in the corner and I'm tired of looking at them. I don't feel like taking care of a home that size anymore. I've been looking for a two bedroom home so I can manage it better. The house has become a time capsule, or a museum with dust."

"Why are you trying to get rid of mom so fast?"

I cleared my throat. "Now watch your tone. This wasn't a fast decision. I still think about her, but I want to start fresh."

She crossed her arms and frowned. "Start fresh?"

"Yes, with a new space. The house is our family home, so I understand you not wanting to let it go. I could sell it to you or put it in a trust so you can rent it out. That would be good money for you, and help pay off school."

"This is too much. Do whatever you want to do, that's what you've been doing." She exhaled loudly.

The server approached again. "Hey family, need some to-go boxes?"

"Yes, please," I said. "For the both of us. I don't think we were as hungry as we thought."

She still gave me a weak hug after leaving but I know she was hurt, that's why I wanted to talk in person rather than text her and ruin her concentration midsemester.

As I was drove home, Tishelle called me.

"Hey, baby. How did hanging out with Genesis and Beatrice go?"

I sighed. "About how I imagined it. We both cried, then I gave her the news about the house and she wasn't happy about it. I want to sell my house, our family house, to her so she can rent it to help pay for college. It's expensive and I don't want her tied to debt. It was a lot for her to process. I hope to see her again before she leaves, but I doubt it. She's probably packing her bag now."

"Oh, darling, it'll be okay. Sometimes it just... takes a minute. Did you want to come over here? I was about to start dinner."

"I'm okay, thank you for asking, sweetheart. I'm just processing myself, too, I guess."

When I got back home I stood in my old bedroom, Bea and I's old bedroom.

Sometimes, I think I can still smell her perfume... like I can now.

I felt a hand on my shoulder but didn't turn around. In my gut, I felt peace after finally telling Genesis the truth finally.

Everything was going to be okay.

17

———

TISHELLE

IT'S BEEN 4 DAYS AND I CAN'T STOP THINKING ABOUT HOW I'VE NEVER seen Vernon's place. What if he has been keeping more secrets? I've been dry in my texts and he's noticed the change so I can't push it anymore. He called me after work and I didn't answer for the first time. When he called me on Friday morning, I decided to put on my big girl panties instead of hiding.

"Hey, Vernon."

"Vernon? You're mad at me? Talk to me, baby. I know it hasn't been long, but you can always talk to me."

"I just don't feel comfortable anymore. I feel like there are secrets." I sighed. Shai was right, he is keeping a secret like how he did for his job.

"What do you want to know about? You can ask anything you want and I'll answer with the truth. Where are you?"

I sighed. "I'm at work."

"Is it okay if I drive over so we can talk? I don't want to take up too much of your time."

"Yea, that's fine I guess."

"I'll be there soon sweetheart."

He pulled into a parking spot right next to my car. I got out and he hugged me tight.

"I missed you, Tishelle. Please tell me what's going on. What did I do? Was it because I brought you to church? I didn't mean to offend you or if it was too much. I never want you to feel forced to do anything."

I shook my head, *that's* what he thought this was about?

"No, no, that's not it. I enjoyed service, I really did. I've been thinking about going back, but I have a problem that only you can solve."

He grabbed my hands. "Tell me and I'll fix it. I don't want to lose you."

The cold breeze hit my cheek and I shivered. "I've never been by your house. You've talked about it, but I've never been there and... it feels like a secret since you've been to mine so many times."

"Sweetheart, I will text you my address right now and you can follow me there right now. I mean it."

I arched my eyebrow. No delaying or lying. He's willing to show me just like that?

"Right now?"

He opened my car door with one hand and his phone in the other texting me.

"Yes, right now." I didn't think we would go right now, just plan it for next week.

I followed his car down the road. I didn't think we would go right now, just him planning it for next week. If someone was there, they would've had time to leave.

Don't go there, hear him out.

As I pulled into the driveway, I was shocked by how big his house was. We were on the west side; a beautiful part of town in a great neighborhood. I wouldn't have minded living here.

We got out of our cars with him leading the way to the front door. "This is it! I want to apologize for the mess before we walk in."

He's a hoarder I knew it!

"It's okay, this is your place."

I walked in and took a deep breath. It was clean and the home smelled like him. I didn't see any clutter, just boxes, like he just moved in. He took me from room to room and each one was filled with boxes except for Genesis', which was moderately clean.

"I see you're ready to move or just moved in."

He sighed. "The rooms have been like this for a while." I wiped my finger on a box and it was covered in dust.

"I see. Where do you sleep?"

We went back down the stairs into an office. One corner had a desk with 2 monitors and the a background I usually saw when we video chatted. A couch sat against the wall, a stripped red and white cane and his line jacket hanging in the corner. On another wall, there were pictures of varying ages with faces I did and didn't recognize. Until one person immediately stood out to me.

"Is this a picture with you and Maynard Jackson?"

He walked behind me, placing his hand on my hip as I leaned onto him. "It is. This is a picture of my mom here," he pointed. "And my siblings here."

There was another family photo with a beautiful woman with curled black hair, a younger looking Vernon, and Genesis maybe 5 years old, looking towards a warm light. "Is this Beatrice?" I asked.

He nodded, still standing close to me, admiring me and the photo. "She's gorgeous. I wish I could've met her." A sweet perfume hit my nose that made me scan the room.

"Yea, that's my Bea. I think she would've liked you, too. She was business minded. I can't believe how big Genesis has gotten. This is her high school graduation photo here. She's changed so much over the last few years. Do you see yourself having a family?" The scent disappeared and I thought of the question he asked me.

There was gentleness and curiosity in his voice. "I could see it, but I'd want to be married. Could you see yourself having more children?"

He laughed loudly. "I don't know if I technically could, but I would never turn my child away, I know what to do with babies better now." He approached a box on his desk. "I need a cigar, want to sit outside with me?"

I haven't seen him smoke since the lounge. He slowly opened the case and brought a cigar to his lips with a matchbox in his hand. We sat outside on the porch, looking at the street. He struck a match against the box and lit it, taking his pull.

"Do you know the reason why I didn't offer my home for you to come by?" He asked as he blew out smoke from his cigar.

I shook my head. I didn't care until more time passed. It was as if Vernon was okay but not okay. I could see his wheels turning now that I'm in 'his space', his house. He's taken care of almost everything I would need, he's fixed so many things around me, including my heart. But when will I fix him? Being there for him at the hospital was easy, I knew he needed me. But how do I keep doing that? Would he even want to be married again? I get it if he doesn't. Genesis is older, but she has her opinions. I don't want him to have to pick between him or me.

"You saw the boxes upstairs? I've been wanting to sell my house. I've been thinking about it but this is the first time I've accepted it. I knew that when you eventually crossed that threshold, it was the last push I needed to sell. I've been looking at places, but not knowing what to look for. But then I saw you smile less than five feet away from me and you've had my heart strings ever since."

I took a deep breath. This was getting serious. He's been there for me, and I want to keep being the person. "If you want to move, then I think you can, baby. I can help with whatever I can."

He stood up. "I got it, baby, I don't want you to worry about it."

I mirrored his actions. "Well, I do because you've been sleeping on a couch. You've paid my rent to make sure I was somewhere comfortable. You deserve to be comfortable and in your own space too."

"Your right sweetheart." He squeezed my hand, "Thank you for reminding me."

"You only slept in a bed when you come over to my place?"

He nodded.

"Let's get you somewhere with a new bed. I don't want your back hurting or anything. I'm glad we didn't come here after dinner or I definitely would have left."

Now he was back laughing and smiling. "I didn't think my house was suitable for guests. You wouldn't have been able to hear me out with the tower of boxes in almost *every* room."

If I never asked, he probably would've never mentioned it. We didn't technically fight about it, I was more... frustrated. Now a 2 ton weight was taken off my chest.

Maybe we are meant to be?

18

VERNON

I NEEDED TISHELLE'S OPINION ON THIS HOUSE BEFORE I SIGNED anything. The owner likes my cash offer, now I just have to get my woman's stamp of approval.

Her car pulled in less than 15 minutes later, she looked around the yard. She was wearing a tan sweater, jeans, and brown boots with a long coat. Her blow out still had some curls at the end. I watched as she noticed the 'For Sale' sign.

"Thinking about buying?"

"Possibly, I wanted to get your thoughts." *Maybe she'll lives here with me one day? Lord willing.*

I enveloped her in a hug and kiss, purposely moving my arms slowly around her back. She grinned up at me. If we weren't in public

I'd pull her into me again for more kisses. She continued admiring the home as she walked closer to the front door. For a split second, I imagined a little girl jumping out of the backseat behind her, with Tishelle's eyes and my skin tone, skipping to the front door in a yellow dress. While Genesis was running to keep up with her little sister.

"Bae! You coming inside?" she called.

My stomach filled with butterflies as she looked back at me. "Yes, coming!" I lightly jogged to the door excited for the future that might come true. I could tell Tishelle was impressed with the architecture as we walked through the layout.

"I like the natural light. This may sound random, but you've done a home inspection including the roof, right?"

I thought about it. "Yea they went on the roof and into the attic. The shingles were installed last year and they did it correctly. I checked myself. Why?" That's a lesson I learned the hard way already.

"I saw a post about a couple skipping the inspection and after living in the new house for a week, a rat fell through a hole in the ceiling. I just realized this is a two bedroom and two and a half bath? Why not get a one bedroom?"

"Just in case Genesis wants to stay over. I'm keeping the bedroom set up, but maybe a different color scheme." *Or a growing family with a woman I've fallen in love with.* "Let me show you the backyard."

We held hands as I opened the sliding doors. "I can close on this house next week. I'll make a few updates and it would be ready to live in soon. I can make the 2nd room your office, with a new desk. You can have as much closet space as you want and I'll make it happen for you. Would you want to live here with me?" I was so excited that I started to ramble.

Her hand paused on my own and she looked at me, confused. "Didn't you just pay my rent until June? I would like to stay in my own place. Always. I know things... aren't great with my business, but I like my apartment. I'm sorry, but no."

I squeezed her hand. It hurt my heart, but I understood. It didn't break my pockets and I wouldn't want the money back. She deserves her own space and I already invade it hanging out in her place all the time. "I apologize. You are right, I got too excited."

I guess the vision was just a dream.

19

TISHELLE

One Month Later

I got out of bed, and stepped on the floor.

SPLASH.

My socks were soaked in water.

The hell?

My feet, carpet, and rug were soaked. My brain couldn't process what was happening. Maintenance came to fix my dishwasher while I took a nap in my room so they could finish and lock up. When I made it to the kitchen, I could see the dishwasher was leaking water like a geyser. I know they fucking saw this. I stood in the kitchen for 30 seconds confused and horrified.

Do something!

I called the office downstairs, no answer. Then I called their emergency line and they said they were on the way. It was only 3 in the afternoon. I called Vernon immediately and told him everything.

"Baby you shouldn't have to live like this. I'll pay for a storage unit for your stuff. A flood is unacceptable. Do you want a hotel or to stay with me?" I heard door closing behind him as he was leaving work.

A hotel? I can only afford that for maybe one night and I'll still need something for the deposit for a new place. If I got a hotel, I'd still ask him to stay with me for a few nights. "You, I want you."

"I'm on the way. I'll take care of it. Fuck your complex, excuse my cursing. I'll be there in 10 minutes if not sooner."

It was like the stress in my body released a little. I just hoped maintenance got here before he did because if not, I knew he'd snap on them.

Eight minutes later, there was a frantic knock at the door. Still shocked from the damage, I opened it. Vernon looked around with concern and anger in his eyes as he took in the floors. "While I work in the kitchen, you start in the closet. If anything is soaked, try to hang it in the bathroom on the curtain rod so the water falls into the tub. Okay?"

I ran back into my room splashing the whole way and cringing. If my suits were ruined, I know I can't afford a new wardrobe. While I was working in the closet, moving my clothes into the bathroom to hang wherever possible. At least 20 minutes passed, Vernon got the dishwasher to stop gushing water around my unit and trying to save my slowly warping kitchen floor. I heard another knock at the door.

Vernon's voice boomed, "Who is it!"

"Maintenance," The man yelled back.

Oh shit. It took them more than 30 minutes to get here. I would've been swimming around my apartment and sweeping water out of my front door looking crazy. As I was walking to the front, I could hear Vernon snapping.

"Man, y'all were supposed to be here 30 minutes ago. My girl's apartment is soaked, Her carpet, her clothes, but you took your time coming up here. This is a water emergency. This could flood downstairs costing, y'all more money. I had to come up here and fix it myself. If I wasn't -"

"Hey..." I interjected. "We did call a while ago."

"I do apologize for the delay, ma'am. Can you show me how far the damage goes?" the man asked, anxiously eyeing Vernon.

"Sure, come with me." I showed him my bedroom and the floor in the bathroom. The only dry place was a small corner of the now empty closet. Was I supposed to sleep in there and ignore the growing mold and smell?

We went back by the front door where Vernon was standing with crossed arms and the meanest look I've ever seen on his face. The maintenance man awkwardly looked between us.

"I'm sorry I didn't get here sooner. We don't have another unit available, so you would be responsible for finding accommodations if you don't want to stay here. I'll come back with a couple of fans."

Vernon opened his mouth immediately, pointing his finger at the man. "After all this, all you can bring is fans?"

I quickly opened the door to let him out and closed the door behind him. I was too tired. Looks like we're headed to Vernon's place, I'm not calling Shai with all this right now.

"Let's just try to fit what we can in my car."

His face softened when he looked at me. "I'm sorry for raising my voice, but he needed to hear it. I can make the trips to the car, just bring what you can to the door.

Two hours later, the fans hummed while blowing air on my furniture and linen as we finished moving my stuff. Now I'm following Vernon to his new house that just so happens to be 15 minutes away from my place. He unloaded the car and moved my stuff into the guest bedroom.

"I still want you to have your own space." I chuckled.

"Yea at least what we brought will survive."

I rubbed my forehead trying not to think about the couch payment I've been ignoring payments on *because* I've been broke. I'm not doing any work tomorrow, I need to go back and see what else I can save.

I'm not giving up that easy.

20

TISHELLE

I'VE BEEN BACK AND FORTH ON THE PHONE WITH MY RENTERS INSURANCE for 3 days. I checked my email and saw that the complex sent me back the funds for my last month's rent through the end of my lease. The few things that weren't soaked was the stuff hanging in my closet and the pans in the kitchen. They found mold, and my lease would be over before the apartment was ready. I deposited it into my account and got a money order. I was just going to give this back to Vernon, since it was technically his money. I'll get more furniture some other way.

When I got back home, Vernon was reading on the back porch. The new yard was smaller than the other house, but enough to look at. Every time I look at new apartments, it makes me miss seeing Vernon every day. I've gotten used to seeing him as easy as walking down the hallway.

I closed the door behind me and looked up I heard, "Hey, baby."

Vernon opened his arms for me and I went to sit on his lap. "Hey, this is for you." I handed him the sealed envelope.

He opened it and looked at the money order with a questioning look.

"Since I didn't want to move to another unit, the complex sent me the money back for my rent. I wanted to return it to you."

"All I'm going to do is deposit it and move it to you. When I paid that, it was a gift to you. I wanted you to have this whether if you're looking for another place or not baby. I mean it." He put his arm around me and squeezed my waist.

Since I moved in, he's made me French vanilla coffee and an English muffins with eggs and sausage every morning. Vernon will sit and rub my feet as I vent about trying to be seen, and being patient for the right opportunity. I just feel like I've reached a dead-end in my business. He and I were talking a few nights ago and I actually spoke out loud about closing Sweet Honey's Marketing Agency. I thought I had what it took, but look at me.

1. No clients
2. No apartment
3. Living with my boyfriend of 2 months

I'm failing at everything lately.

THE NEXT DAY IN MY OFFICE, AS MY SPACE HEATER BLEW WARM AIR ON my feet, my computer suddenly rang with an unknown number. I wasn't about to answer it. My mind was swarming with thoughts about everything. Then, my gut screamed *"girl put on a fake smile and answer the phone!"*

"Hello?" I answered.

"Hi, Tishelle! You may not remember me, but we met briefly at the Mayors Holiday Gala. How are you doing today?"

I cleared my throat. "I'm good, what about you?" I met so many people that night it was a blur.

"Oh I'm fine. Look, I'm calling because I wanted to ask you a question. I'm a member of the board for a confidential tech company here in California. We really need a marketing analyst to come in and be a major partner in our change initiative. We have this document we've been to get clients, but it hasn't done the trick."

She shared her screen, and the flyer looked like it was done in Windows XP. It was grainy and honestly didn't look real.

"Mmm, at first glance, there is a lot of page real estate that can be utilized. I can not only clean this up for you, but make you stand out against the competitors in Silicon Valley. Whether if you need a new look, advertisement ideas, communication and social media plan."

"Perfect! I knew you had the eye for this. We need a real revamp with marketing, strategy, and product enhancements throughout the whole organization. So this would take a series of months and juggling multiple priorities, but you really stand out in the crowd. Can we start negotiations with an 18-month contract at $250,000?"

I started coughing and holding my chest. *Lord, hold on! This is a negotiation.* You never take the first number they offer.

"I would love the opportunity to work with your company. I have multiple years of marketing and project management experience. I have some reference feedback I can provide to showcase the pristine work of my agency. Do you have room to go up to $280,000? I already have a great idea to directly impact your target market."

I could hear the pause but I waited for her to speak first. I don't remember meeting this woman and $250,000 is more than enough to get straight.

"Yea! And were open to extending the contract if needed. Meeting you in person, then hearing of your achievements, you're the candidate we need. We have our ways of knowing how great and exceptional you are. We are looking forward to this partnership. We'll send your contract by the end of the day today. How long would you need to review it and add suggestions to the document?"

I scribbled on my notepad, "48 to 72 hours is enough for me. Thank you so much for considering me for this! I'm really looking forward to taking your business to the next level."

"Same for us. Please let me know if you need anything else or have suggestions for contract changes."

This contract literally couldn't have come at a better time. I texted

Shai and my mom the great news. Nothing like an *"I got a job!"* text. Shai sent a video of her twerking in front of her oven while my mom sent a series of crying, smiling, and dancing emojis.

I made it back home, I mean Vernon's house, and couldn't wait to tell him the good news. "Hey, bae! I have some great news but tell me about your day first."

"I'm just reading over these water test results and making comparisons. Everything looks good, but you can never be too sure. I also saved our tails on a quote because they were trying to get us to pay 35% up front. I'm talking them down to 15% minimum since I found multiple discrepancies in the fine print of our invoices. This contract has some fixes before any pen touches that paper."

I brushed my finger across his chest. "You better tell them! Reading is fundamental, save that money. Speaking of money, I got a high paying client! And secured a nice contract today." I couldn't stop myself from hopping up and down.

He sat up in excitement. "Okay, baby! See look, I told you it was around the corner. How nice?"

"Over $200K."

"Congratulations!" He wrapped me in a tight hug as we spun in his chair. "You deserve it. I'm so proud of you. Let's go out to dinner to celebrate."

I don't know why, but the thought of going somewhere for dinner disgusted me. I suddenly went from super excited to drained. Honestly, I don't feel like getting dressed and putting on real clothes. I know my period is around the corner. I just feel so gross.

"Can we just stay in tonight? We're already going out for Valentine's Day next week and don't want anything too big."

He kissed my cheek, "Whatever you want, baby. This is your night and we're going to celebrate you however you want. Is there anything you have a taste for?"

"Marinated beef tacos and strawberry margaritas."

He stood up from the chair. "I'm going to make a run really quick. How about you just stay in the bedroom until I tell you to come out?

You can lay down and take a quick nap. You need rest and *not* scroll on your phone."

"Ooo, you're surprising me?" I gave a half smile.

He nodded, pulling me in with an imaginary rope. "Yes because you have been working hard creating those connections and your work speaks for itself. Now, go lay down and put your feet up."

When I stood up and walked past him, he smacked my ass. I made my way to 'my room' until he came to get me.

21

VERNON

A night in with tacos? Easy. Anything for my baby. I hate that she's not feeling good. I hope a bug isn't making its way around.

I have to do something nice for her to celebrate. I may have nudged someone in her direction. When an old friend and I ran into each other at the gala, I knew Tishelle could set him back on course. She was her usual glowing and conversational self. After a reminder, he decided to take her on. I may have nudged him in her direction but she still earned it. He reached out to her previous clients, and they only said great things about her and her work ethic. I'm proud of her for everything she has worked hard for.

"Cover your eyes."

She chuckled while squeezing her eyes shut. I still covered her eyes with my hand as we walked out to the living room. I was anxious to see her reaction.

I knew to buy a new couch. The pieces of this one can maneuver into an queen size bed, just in case an extra guest stays over. I added even more pillows, covered in blankets and sheets, surrounded by warm, yellow Christmas lights. It was an elevated fort with cookies and cream ice cream, tacos, and margaritas expertly placed.

"Okay, open them," I said moving my hand down.

She gasped, and from the smile growing on her face I could tell she loved it.

"Wow, Vernon... wow! Not even an hour passed and you've got drinks waiting for us. This is really cute and thoughtful." She lightly kissed my lips and cheek. "I love you."

"I love you, too." I said with no hesitation as I looked at her in admiration. She finally said what I've been feeling since the night we met. I walked over to the couch and grabbed our glasses.

"To my *especially* successful girlfriend. I'm so proud of you and the hard work you continue doing. Not only are you the best at your job but you're exceptional in every way. Congratulations on this contract and to many more to come."

"I'm the only person in my business," she said with a chuckle. "But thank you so much. To many more," we clinked our glasses. "I like how you always step up no matter what. You keep showing me how much you care about me and relax me. I really deserved this."

"You deserve this and so much more." We took a sip and winced. "Mmm, at least you know they didn't leave the most important ingredient out."

I laughed. "That is true, baby."

We watched a comedy while we devoured our food and drinks. When we finished and I cleaned up while Tishelle dozed off in the corner with pile of pillows. She looked so peaceful as she lightly snored.

I slowly bent down, scooping her up in my arms and placing her in my bed-our bed. She took a deep breath of the pillows and smiled in her sleep. "I'm finally in here." She mumbled. "Good night. I love you."

"I love you, too, baby."

That night was the best night of sleep I'd gotten since the cabin trip.

22

TISHELLE

Valentine's Day

Looking across the table adorned in red roses, Vernon sat holding my hand across the table. From the first week of December to now, he's done everything he said he would. He made me his girlfriend, spoiled me, and made me smile in so many ways. My skin is glowing, we've been getting along since moving in, and he doesn't let anything worry me, like a gentleman. Everything seems so smooth and... almost perfect. With the house being so intimate, it's like our own fairytale. I've never told him to take out the trash, or wash the dishes. He just does it. I do my fair share of chores, too, but he's taking care of himself, Genesis, and me. There is a lot on his shoulders, and he's been balancing it well.

Roswell and Lashai were at a table not far from us laughing and also holding hands. Whenever my eyes would catch hers, she would smile and shrug. Will she take Roswell seriously? I'm not sure yet. But I do know that I plan to be with Vernon for a while.

My plate of baked fish was placed in front of me and my stomach immediately turned. I could feel the fluid rising up my throat.

"Excuse me," I quickly said before standing up and running into the bathroom, gagging. I pushed through the door, entered the first stall I saw, and threw up into the toilet. I couldn't even close the door behind me before everything I ate came back up in horrible heaves. The worst thing was the smell of the toilet fumes, which just made me throw up more.

How can I smell someones perfume right now, on top of everything else hitting my nose?

As I was gasping for air I heard the door close behind me and shoes coming closer to the stall door.

"Yes, she's fine," I heard Lashai say. Then I felt her hand pulling back my hair and rubbing my back. "Oh no, the food didn't sit right?"

I coughed into the toilet again. "I didn't even get to eat it. The smell of the fish made me nauseous. If I didn't run in here I would've thrown up at the table."

Her hand paused on my back. "The smell of it?" she asked.

"Oh, fuck. I was supposed to get my period 2 weeks ago."

Shai chuckled behind me, still rubbing my back. "So, you had big fun in that cabin. This is going to make the rest of your dinner *very* interesting. I hope he likes this unforgettable Valentine's gift."

Oh. My. Gosh.

The End

ABOUT THE AUTHOR

Kirahvi is a captivating romance author who transforms everyday moments into extraordinary love stories. She crafts heart-stopping contemporary romances that explore the beautiful complexity of modern relationships.

From steamy airport reunions to quiet, bookish encounters in cozy bars, her novels blend heart-fluttering passion with relatable characters chasing their dreams-and sometimes each other.

Kirahvi is also a Florida born and Georgia living author that loves love. Throughout her childhood, Kirahvi spent her free time writing heartfelt poems and short stories in fictional lands. After graduating with an MBA, she fell deeper in love with the romance genre. When not recording for her BookTube, she's at a museum, park or listening to a vinyl record. She is married to her high school sweetheart and the family waves their Buccaneers flag high!

Follow her on Instagram, TikTok, YouTube, Threads and Facebook on @Kirahvi_ReadsnWrites or visit her website www.kirahvibel lo.com for more information about her and events coming soon.

Don't forget to leave your review on Amazon, Goodreads and/or StoryGraph! Every review helps support indie authors!